Didda

A trailblazer and a maverick business leader across media and entertainment spectrum is the easiest introduction to **Ashish Kaul**. Not only has he implemented path-breaking business successes but also created a space for himself as an advocacy columnist. He represents a bold new generation of mavericks who refuse to be stereotyped and have etched their own histories. Ashish Kaul is among the brave new breed of multilingual writers who believe that content has the power to create women friendly societies that will lead to a stronger India. Ashish's Hindi novel on Kashmir titled *Refugee Camp* has been extremely successful.

Reach him at:
https://www.facebook.com/ashishrattankaul
Twitter @aashishkaul
Instagram @aashishkaul

Didda
The Warrior Queen of Kashmir

ASHISH KAUL

Published by
Rupa Publications India Pvt. Ltd 2019
7/16, Ansari Road, Daryaganj
New Delhi 110002

Sales centres:
Allahabad Bengaluru Chennai
Hyderabad Jaipur Kathmandu
Kolkata Mumbai

Copyright © Ashish Kaul 2019

The views and opinions expressed in this book are the author's
own and the facts, as reported by him, are based on extensive research
as well as oral accounts by the descendants of Didda, including the
author's grandmother. The facts have been verified to the extent possible,
and the author and publishers are not in any way liable for the same.
Some creative liberties have been taken in the author's narration of
events and characters.

All rights reserved.
No part of this publication may be reproduced, transmitted,
or stored in a retrieval system, in any form or by any means,
electronic, mechanical, photocopying, recording or otherwise,
without the prior permission of the publisher.

First impression 2019

ISBN: 978-93-5333-378-2

10 9 8 7 6 5 4 3 2 1

Printed in HT Media Ltd., Gr. Noida

This book is sold subject to the condition that it shall not,
by way of trade or otherwise, be lent, resold, hired out, or otherwise
circulated, without the publisher's prior consent, in any form of binding or
cover other than that in which it is published.

Contents

Author's Note	*vii*
Foreword	*ix*
Gratitude	*xv*

1.	Birth of the Queen and the Prophecy	1
2.	The Curse of Vitasta and the Dark Prophecy	40
3.	The Sorcerer, the Death and the Birth of the King	57
4.	The Battle of Pattan and the Practice of Sati	78
5.	The Temple Siege and the Rise of the Ekangi's	89
6.	The New Prince and the Regent	108
7.	Narvahan's Death and the End of an Era	131
8.	Didda and the Bride from Himavat	142
9.	The Monk Queen and Tunga—the New Army Commander	186
10.	Didda's Final Tryst with Destiny and the Sultan of Ghaznavi	200

Author's Note

History has always been unkind, unscrupulous and cruel to women. Didda was no exception. It has always been difficult to accept powerful women.

Almost 1,200 years separate our generation from the life and times of Didda. No one can be sure of who she really was, as she transcended from being a young girl, craving for the love of her parents, to a warrior and a queen who ruled for the longest time in the history of the mediaeval world. Many gallant warriors and men of power have since come and gone. They ravaged the northern territories and rewrote the histories that were convenient to them. Somewhere amongst those cowards, a great queen was lost in the sands of time until now.

Didda has kept me awake for years, since I heard her name from my illustrious grandmother who hailed from the lineage of the families who once ruled Paranotsa, now Poonch.

However, history has had a few mentions of Didda—born of SimhRaj, the ruler of the mighty Lohar dynasty. She was married off to a debauched king of Kashmir, KshemGupt, as no one was willing to marry her.

Didda, who belonged to a rare breed of individuals, transcended from being an ordinary girl to a legend in her own lifetime.

While history was continuously being erased, rewritten or forgotten, a few fragments fell off and lay hidden, until I discovered them. No one can claim to know the entire truth—the story of a girl, abandoned into the care of servants, rising to become one of the greatest queens who unified a fragmented land mass to build one of the largest kingdoms, after Lalitaditya the Great.

However, Didda has remained hidden in the hearts of the people. All her admirers, as well as detractors, have their version of her story to tell. Some have hated her for being cruel and ruthless, while others, like me, have fallen in love with her for doing what she believed was right. For some, she has been an extraordinary woman, but for others, especially the powerful men who couldn't defeat her, she was a witch.

For years, I struggled to put the pieces together, going on for days, weeks and even months without proper sleep. Eventually, I began to see her in my dreams, holding my hand and telling me who she was, narrating the story that has travelled far beyond the realm of modern times, screaming to be set free.

This is my story of hers!

Ashish Kaul

Foreword

Didda—A Bewitching Story That Needs to be Told

An overview of world history reconfirms that women have been accorded an ornamental status at best. Vedic India has imbued women with exemplary substance, but consequent invasions and regimes altered, and mostly eradicated, such history to establish a male sociocultural dominance. The truth, however, seeps in through the window, if one closes the doors, and so does our story.

Our story, buried for over 1,200 years, details the courage, valour and sacrifices of a woman who was abandoned by her parents and married off to a debauched king. She survived being pushed into the practice of sati, and crushed the mutiny led by a powerful prime minister. She rose above life's challenges and her physical disability to become the greatest and the longest-serving queen in the history of the mediaeval world. She created a space for herself in a period that was dominated by powerful men and kings who refused to be ruled by a woman and that too, with a disability. Such was her valour that she would alter the fate of battles and scare deadly warlords into submission. In fact, they were so scared of her that they believed she was a witch.

When we talk of powerful women in Indian political history,

a name which never surfaces is that of Didda's—the queen of Kashmir. Didda is the untold story of a physically-disabled woman steeped into a life of solitary struggles and destined to become queen. This is the story of Didda's classical emergence to power—apart from the submissive feminine life of bearing male heirs to the throne—to become Kashmir's ruler for fifty-four years (950–1003). During her reign, she took Kashmir to vibrant peaks and left it as the most powerful kingdom in mediaeval Asia.

Didda was born to King SimhRaj and Queen Shreelekha in AD 925. Born with a disability, or perhaps affected by polio at birth, she walked with a limp.

Didda survived an attack at birth and grew up in the capital city of Loharin of the Lohar kingdom that ruled most of the northwest of undivided Vedic India. She grew up in an environment of ridicule and was deprived of parental love. The other children in the palace often made fun of her disability. She had no one to turn to until Valaga, a maid, came into her life. Valaga looked after Didda selflessly and became her companion and confidante. The love and affection that Didda sought from her parents eventually came from Valaga.

Didda was an exceptionally gifted child; she was intelligent, an inspirational orator and, despite her physical disability, she loved to sprint. Such was her passion for life that she would participate in the palace games and run to win in them with the help of her chaperone, Valaga. A spectacle as such is unheard of anywhere in the world.

Despite her abilities, it had become impossible for the king to find a groom for Didda as no one wanted to marry a lame girl. Deep inside, she was falling apart and when the time came to get married to a king notorious for his debauchery, she seized the opportunity and made the best of it. After her marriage to King KshemGupt of Kashmir, she realized that his kingdom was in disarray and on the verge of collapse due to the depraved king. Didda began to take political decisions and soon became the centre of governance despite strong opposition from the prime minister and his daughter who was also KshemGupt's first wife. Once she established a foothold in the kingdom, she went on to control the entire empire. She was able to galvanize support from other ministers and implemented major reforms that won her public support. The main reason for Didda's command and control was the support of the king, as she had given him a legitimate heir, which no one else could.

After the sudden death of the king in AD 950, Didda was at a crossroads. She was threatened by a mutiny led by the prime minister and faced hostility from all. The prime minister, along with other key ministers, wanted to force Didda to perform sati so that he could take over the throne. She initially agreed but came out of the situation with the help of a trusted minister, Narvahan. She then anointed her young son Abhimanyu, as king.

Attempts to kill Didda continued, but they only made her stronger by the day. Didda led from the front and she, herself, fought in many battles alongside her soldiers, which won their support. However, the nobles and other kings did not want to be ruled by a woman, and that too, one with a disability; thus, the rebellions continued.

Didda, by then, had transformed from a girl into a warrior and realized that until she crushed them all, those powerful men would not let her live in peace. She went on to recall her gallant and trusted trainer, VikramSen, to constitute one of the deadliest combat units in the world called the 'Ekangi's'. Didda appointed Narvahan as the prime minister and expanded the empire under his command. Over time, Narvahan became enamoured of Didda and love blossomed. But, when Didda realized this, she cut off her interactions with him and a distraught Narvahan committed suicide.

Meanwhile, she arranged Abhimanyu's marriage with a beautiful princess, Vasundhara. Abhimanyu was a simpleton who got carried away by the charms of his wife. Vasundhara saw Didda as a threat and knew that as long as Didda was in the palace, she would not be as powerful. She began to poison Abhimanyu's mind against Didda and he began to rebel against his mother. Eventually, Abhimanyu forced Didda out of the palace and she renounced the world, living the life of a monk in the outskirts of the palace.

After Abhimanyu's premature demise, Vasundhara tried to take over the throne. Didda, once again, marched back and took over the reins of the kingdom. She saw the turmoil created due to Abhimanyu's inept administration and worked hard to restore order in the kingdom.

Didda had become bitter because of the continuous conspiracies and betrayals, and closed her heart to love. The only thing that mattered to Didda the most was the integrity of her kingdom. However, Didda eventually developed a liking for her saviour, a herdsman named Tunga. She inducted him into the court but soon realized that her fondness for him was becoming an impediment to her rule. With the growing assassination attempts on Tunga, she decided to shift him to Lohar to help her brother.

Not only did Didda overcome her disability and hold together a kingdom that was on the verge of disintegration, she also created a much larger empire and an administration that ushered prosperity for her people. With her foresight, she developed strong border administration alongside the northeast and defeated Ghazni twice with her strategies. In her lifespan of seventy-nine years, Didda became an enigma and an icon that sent shivers down her enemies' spines. People saw Didda as a cold-hearted, cruel woman, not realizing that she had sacrificed a lot to build a vast kingdom to fulfil the last wish of her dying husband.

Didda was no ordinary woman, and it goes without saying that her life was nothing short of extraordinary. It was marked by trials and tribulations, victories, love, wit and passion. Mediaeval folklore represents any woman, who has emerged to such heights during this era dominated by powerful kings, as a witch. Beyond a shadow of doubt, retelling Didda's bewitching tale as the longest reigning queen against odds would grip and hook audiences. Above all, it is also in accord with the wave of feminism that dominates our times.

The author has gone to great lengths to create an unforgettable story of India's forgotten history. The entire story has been written in a manner that makes it an effortless, yet a gripping read. More so, the characters are endearing and real which make them even more engaging.

Didda is a story that will change historical perspectives. I believe the author is the first to undertake such a Herculean task and bring an invaluable piece of our history to life by recreating a story that was buried and forgotten for over 1,200 years. I envied western authors who have written amazing epic stories and wondered when a culturally rich country like India would produce a masterpiece. Didda is India's major beginning. Hers is a story that will break global stereotypes. It is a story that needs to be told. Didda is not just a story, but also the spirit of women. It is a testimony that the women of the world will not bow down to the tyranny of history written by weak men in power. They will rise and take their rightful place, for Didda has awakened.

Deepa Malik
Padmashree and Arjuna Awardee
Silver Medalist, Rio Paralympics, 2016
President's First Ladies Award, 2018
President's National Role Model, 2014
IPC Asian Record F53 (Javelin)
Niti Ayog Women Transformation Award
Femina Women's Award—Sports, 2017
4 Limca World Records (Adventure)
Motivational Speaker
A proud mother and the wife of an Army man

Gratitude

To Didda, who continues to live in the extraordinary women of all times. Sometimes, crippled by the men in power and often abandoned by her own blood, she rises time and again as some remarkable women like Shefali Chaturvedi, Sanjali Shirodkar, Sarita Kaul, my maternal grandmother Smt Sobhagyawati Kilam and my mother Pushpa Kaul.

Thank you all for keeping Didda alive.

Thank you, Shereen, for coming into my life!

Thank you, world, for forgetting Didda for 1,200 years, so that I could find her, again.

Thank you, Sudha Verma, for designing the cover of *Didda: The Warrior Queen of Kashmir*.

1

Birth of the Queen and the Prophecy

AD 925: The Kashmir Kingdom, Northern Frontiers

The sun is about to drown into the mesmerizing expanse of an enigmatic lake. Autumn has announced itself in Kashmir and the chinars seem to be engulfed in fire. From afar, the flames are reaching out to the skies, as if to douse a fire deep within. A royal boat is wading through the still waters of Lake Satisar. It has a fluttering crimson flag with an unmissable sign of the third eye of Lord Shiva and the crescent moon. A royal boat, with two kings aboard, was a rare sight in Kashmir. Both the kings appear to be in deep thought and seem eager to reach the shore. Suddenly, a strong gust of wind breaks their contemplation and their anxiety paves way for fear. The kings look up at the mast and find the flag fluttering in the opposite direction. Both of them, still silent and consumed by an unknown fear, hold on to the flagstaff. Sweat beads appear on their foreheads as the waters start churning. The boatmen begin to scream and so do the kings as a whirlpool creeps from within the lake and rises to the flag. The screams of the kings and the pawns on the boat freeze with fear. After a moment of deafening crescendo, a noxious calm descends and stills everything around as something begins to appear from within the frozen heart of the mystical lake.

The ghastly expressions on the kings' faces turn disquiet as flames begin to emerge from the waters, dancing atop the golden crisp leaves of the four trees planted by the gods themselves on the floating island of Char Chinari.

The earthly abode of Kashyap—the creator of the kingdom of Kashmir—had not been seen in a long while as no one from the long legacy of warrior kings had dared to visit the island, until now. The waters of the lake dance around the island as if in a symphony, cascading into the waters. An alluring ball of light begins to take shape atop a mound as the kings disembark cautiously on the sacred grounds below. The royal boat stands still and so do the boatmen as if frozen in a surreal painting—even the royal flag has slumped or maybe it is scared to be noticed by the curious eyes. The alluring ball bursts into shards of tiny twinkles and a sanyasi, or saint, appears with his eyes closed. The kings begin their journey of, what seems like, a million miles towards him.

The sanyasi's facial expressions begin to change with every step the kings take. His eyebrows begin to furrow, and the calmness makes way for trauma as the kings appear in front of him.

The sanyasi opens his eyes and shouts, 'Oh king! Your son would be of no good...no good!'

A sudden roar builds up in the lake and the rest of his words could not be heard. The sanyasi closes his eyes once more, and his body begins to tremble and change its form.

His fingers transmute into claws and his hair into stripes. Both the kings take a step back and start retreating to the boat. A ferocious tiger now stands in place of the sanyasi. He roars and pounces on the kings.

A loud scream echoes across the lake, and precipitously, King KshemGupt wakes up with sweat on his forehead.

He had been having this dream for a while. Two kings on a royal boat and the emblem of the third eye of Lord Shiva? It was the insignia of the Kashmir dynasty he was ruling, but who were the two kings, the sanyasi and the tiger? KshemGupt clapped his hands, a signal for the personal attendants to come in.

The pradhan sewak informed the king that Minister Narvahan and Prime Minister Phalgun seek an audience with the king. KshemGupt frowned at the sewak but didn't say anything. He was still entangled in the thoughts of his dream. The sewak waited for a signal, the usual nod, from the king to usher in Narvahan and Phalgun.

'The jackals must be missing me; I could hear them howling all night,' said KshemGupt. He knew it was time for him to get ready for the hunt. It was clear that he was not ready to address the kingdom or its issues.

KshemGupt moved towards the wide balcony—Zoon Dab—as his mother used to call it because of the beautiful and uninterrupted view of the full moon it offered. There were no more full moon nights of his childhood though, as the kingdom was waning. The once regal clamours of prosperity that echoed across the vast expanse of Srinagaram, the capital city of Kashmir, were heard no more.

Srinagaram had galvanized itself along the banks of the sacred river Vitasta that played an imperative role in the daily lives of every soul living in the capital and the entire kingdom. The view, however, had not waned as far as KshemGupt's memory served. His thoughts were interrupted by a rally of sewaks (male servants or attendants) walking in to prime the king with the royal attire. Alongside the sewaks, strode Narvahan—his closest friend, confidant and minister. KshemGupt seemed to relax in the company of Narvahan. Not only had they grown up together, but also over the years, Narvahan had offered unconditional sanity to his seemingly brazen life. KshemGupt depended on Narvahan more for compassion than counsel, which was primarily left to Phalgun—the prime minister of Kashmir. While Narvahan kneeled before KshemGupt with his everlasting smile, Phalgun stood in the foreground wearing an expression of profound disdain for this friendship.

'Damars have rebelled again, my king,' Phalgun's voice echoed across the chamber disturbing the brief calm and serenity. 'I am told that Damars are uniting and this is likely to transform into a civil unrest,' Phalgun continued, further cleansing the shards of a smile.

'Did you hear the jackals, Phalgun? I wonder what has been keeping them up all night.'

Phalgun stood sterile, unaffected, expecting the banter.

'Perhaps the jackals can sense the impending danger for my king,' Phalgun continued with the banter.

Narvahan turned towards Phalgun and asked, 'Do you mock the king, Phalgun?'

Narvahan's thunderous response reflected his passion and loyalty towards his king and friend. However, Phalgun was not perturbed in any way. He could not be for he was who he was—

the most powerful minister Kashmir had ever had. A descendant of the noble bloodline of Brahmin warlords, Phalgun had played an important role in the churning of Kashmir; a churning that had changed the ruling dynasty. Phalgun came from the lineage of loyal ministers who had served the erstwhile kings of the Lalitaditya's dynasty. Even when SangramDev was removed by ParvGupt, he retained a young Phalgun as a key minister. His administrative and leadership abilities surpassed his age even then. ParvGupt, however, didn't have the keen eye to look deep into the hearts of men with dark souls. Phalgun's greatest stimulus was his ambition, which he guarded deep inside and surrounded it by a lace of chivalry and resolute demeanour.

Kashmir was going through turbulent times with rebellions from powerful Damars across the kingdom. Damars were not always rebellious but peace-loving landlords. Sixty years ago, they had been driven to the brink of chaos by the erstwhile King SangramDev. KshemGupt's father, ParvGupt, had tried his best to restore peace with them and did achieve a phase of harmony. Damars across the region had been victims of deep-rooted corruption that ailed the kingdom and ran across the civil administration. Hence, their war was against corruption and not with the state. ParvGupt had tried his best to cleanse his administration and provide a reformed social structure to all the classes encompassing the all-powerful Damars and had been successful to some extent. However, the irony of the situation in Kashmir was the manner in which the wheel of time had turned and now, sixty years later, Kashmir found itself entangled in the same complex web of corruption and anarchy that ParvGupt and Phalgun had fought to eradicate. Now, by ignoring Damars, KshemGupt brought Kashmir back to where

SangramDev had left it. After King ParvGupt passed away, the subsequent increase in taxes prompted them to close the ranks and revolt once again.

KshemGupt was never interested in administration as his passion lay somewhere else—somewhere that even he wasn't sure of. He seemed to be chasing a dream that he could not decipher. 'Am I cruel?' was something he often asked Narvahan. After his coronation, KshemGupt had not even been on the customary rounds of the kingdom, not even to Srinagaram—the capital city.

Phalgun stared at KshemGupt with an unwavering gaze while the sewaks primed the king. Soon, the king excused them and turned to Narvahan, perhaps attempting to render Phalgun debilitated, and told him that such uprisings were a distraction to his pleasures and must be quelled. However, Narvahan begged to differ. He believed rampant corruption and absence of justice fuelled the uprisings.

On his part, Phalgun was repulsed with the king's statements, but he did not lose his composure for he knew the danger of crossing the line, given the eccentric temperament of the king.

Narvahan also knew that KshemGupt didn't have a bone for the welfare of Kashmir, but as a friend and a minister of the state, he felt compelled to remind the king of his duties. Narvahan had been doing this for a while now and he knew KshemGupt was born rudderless, and the king would continue to be what he was until he found his true purpose.

'And, we must not forget the curse too… It seems to be the time,' Narvahan spoke unobtrusively. While KshemGupt didn't hear a word, Phalgun's eyes turned sharply towards Narvahan.

He walked swiftly towards KshemGupt and urged the king to leave the quelling to him.

'Quelling?' Narvahan appeared perturbed. KshemGupt turned towards Phalgun and looked deep into his eyes.

'I mustn't be distracted, Phalgun; the jackals don't let me sleep,' KshemGupt, preoccupied with his vices, didn't realize the dreadful plot unfurling at the behest of Phalgun. Unaware of Phalgun's dark desires, KshemGupt happily gave the responsibility to him, while a disappointed Narvahan looked on. Phalgun stared at the king and wondered, 'How could a man be so remorseless? Was it because KshemGupt was in a game without any stake?'

What Phalgun couldn't see was destiny, quietly laughing in a corner, because in the not so distant future, the word 'remorseless' was going to take a new meaning. The wheel of time had begun to turn to fulfil SangramDev's unfinished business.

Armed with the king's order, Phalgun set out to quell the rebellions ruthlessly. He set their crops on fire and plundered their barns in village after village, all along the banks of Vitasta. Public hangings of the rebels became an evening leisure and decapitated heads donned the spikes as a reminder that Phalgun had been there. Phalgun unleashed a terror that reminded every soul of SangramDev. Outnumbered and broken, the Damars retreated into submission. Some of them felt indignant, as the promised saviour of Srinagaram had not arrived. They wondered whether it was all a lie. However, how could Dev Rishi Kashyap be so wrong?

While KshemGupt was seeking peace amidst the jackals, Phalgun was almost done rendering Vitasta into cerise and Kashmir was engulfed in a demonic haze.

KshemGupt soon returned to the palace to indulge in orgies, Kathak with the select courtesans known as *hoors*, or celestial beauties. Hoors were brought from many parts of the kingdom and some even from far-off lands. They had to have heavy bosoms for KshemGupt liked to have his daily dose of bahuvadini, or bhang, mixed with freshly milled Kashmiri almond-laced milk, straight off their bare bodies. The after effects of this had been taking a toll on his harem as, in a rage, he would often bite off their nipples. The hoors would yell in pain and KshemGupt would immerse himself in the pleasure of their screams. Often, he would confuse the taste of blood with that of bahuvadini. Narvahan knew that for KshemGupt, the fine line between pain and pleasure had blurred. It wasn't unusual for KshemGupt to be oblivious to his surroundings, and it was usually left to Narvahan to manage the durbar, or court.

The king was enjoying one such performance when Phalgun walked into the royal durbar with a head on a spike and a victorious smile on his face. 'My king, I give you Vrajeshwar Dev.' He placed the head at the king's feet. Vrajeshwar Dev was touted as the strongest Damar warlord, and his head meant the voices had been silenced.

Narvahan along with other members of the royal court were in shock. The blood dripped from the decapitated head. KshemGupt stood up—a rare moment—and with him stood the entire court. He stepped down his throne. He looked at the head with distaste and gave out a loud cry of victory, kicking the skull out of his way. Narvahan stood frozen, defeated by the demons that now possess the man who was once his dearest friend. KshemGupt placed both his hands on Phalgun's shoulders, for

Birth of the Queen and the Prophecy 9

it was a moment to celebrate. He told Phalgun, 'I also kept my end of the bargain; the jackals have been quiet for a while.'

Phalgun smiled, 'And, I kept mine. We are a team, my king!'

KshemGupt told Phalgun that he was worthy of a reward, which made Phalgun nervous. This was the moment that Phalgun had been waiting for since eternity. KshemGupt sensed this rare anxiety and asked Phalgun if he doubted the king's intent. A sheepish Phalgun attempted a feeble yet cautioned laughter, 'No, my king. It was just that I had a dream. They don't come true, do they?'

'Don't they, Phalgun? In Kashmir, there is a God above and KshemGupt below, and all is well in heaven.'

'I want my Chandralekha to serve the throne, my king.'

'Serve the throne?' KshemGupt seemed amused.

'Serve as your consort, my king. I want her to serve the throne as the queen of Kashmir.'

Silence gripped the court and Narvahan felt a chill run down his spine. Was it time for the dark prophecy to come true?

Narvahan and everyone else were sure that Phalgun would seek a fair share of the kingdom that he had once lost to the former king. Phalgun's proposal of a marriage of his enchanting daughter, Chandralekha, with the king, as the prize for his service to the throne, left everyone in awe of Phalgun's abilities as the prime minister and a diplomat. With this act of genius, Phalgun travelled a million miles across two dynasties. However, the big question that remained unanswered was— why would he want his one and only beloved daughter married off to a debased king? The quiet and cautious footsteps in the corridors of the grand palace gave way to whispers. The entire court knew of the moral vagaries of the king and his harem full of women, including the consorts of some of the ministers.

They all knew of the king's penchant for women and the numerous concubines that lay bare in his harem. That is why they could not understand why Phalgun would want his only daughter—the daughter he raised all alone after the death of his wife—be betrothed to a debauched king?

Among those curious faces was a scared face of Narvahan. A storm was brewing deep inside him. The harsh winter skyline of Kashmir was paving way for a beautiful spring, but Narvahan was wilting and hoping KshemGupt would turn down the proposal. All eyes were set on the king. With bated breaths, all of them waited for the king's decision.

Even though KshemGupt had not seen Chandralekha in a while, he remembered how beautiful she was. She was sensuous, white as milk, and had a voluptuous figure that any man would be attracted to. The king, unaware of the dark ploy, agreed to marry Chandralekha; thus, cementing Phalgun's position in the kingdom and almost inciting the consequence.

Phalgun was gazing at the sunset across the vast expanse of Vitasta from his chamber as Chandralekha walked in. She was agitated and resentful as she looked at Phalgun with a million thoughts racing through her mind. She wasn't sure if she was looking at the same man who was her doting father. Was her father and Prime Minister Phalgun different men? If not, then who was this man who used to sing her to sleep after her mother died, and now had decided to burn down her dreams.

Phalgun looked at Chandralekha's furrowed brows on her forehead, the same forehead he kissed every morning. He walked up to her and gestured her maids to leave them. Before Chandralekha could speak, Phalgun told her that he had waited for this day for over eighteen years. He explained that he should have been the king, but the circumstances had been so compelling that he chose to forsake his dream. 'A son would have made a difference then and another one will make a difference now,' continued Phalgun.

Looking back at Vitasta, he said, 'It was more than SangramDev that the Vitasta had swallowed and it is about time my share bellows out of her womb.'

Chandralekha stood there quietly, staring with her stoic and soulful eyes making pain look beautiful. She realized that it was not her father but a conniving, desolate man and his demonic ambition standing before her. But then, he was also the same man who, like any other father in the world, had held her tiny fingers and taught her the meaning of life. A daughter's love for her father had no parallel, no matter how depraved he is—he was still her daughter's hero. Chandralekha was no different and she ran into her father's reassuring embrace. A forgotten dark prophecy seemed to be coming alive and Phalgun believed this marriage had brought him closer to the throne.

In AD 950, the royal palace of Srinagaram was decorated like never before. Chandralekha became the queen of hearts, quite literally, and strode deep into the heart of the palace and KshemGupt. The wedding night was special too as Narvahan had ordered the royal boat to be decorated like a queen and the bed was prepared out of the freshly-plucked Kashmiri roses. The fragrance of the roses reached out to the palace as the night grew. Phalgun could smell the fragrance and he knew the seeds of future were being planted in the womb of time. It was now just a long wait, not only for Phalgun but for every soul of Kashmir. The only difference—for Phalgun, it was the throne of Srinagaram, and for everyone else, it was for their promised saviour.

In AD 952, KshemGupt had been married for two years and Chandralekha had become a mother of two beautiful daughters, but she had not been able to provide an heir to the throne. This had upset KshemGupt and, more importantly, Phalgun. So near, yet so far from the throne, Phalgun's desires had now begun to consume him from within. He decided to not wait anymore; he summoned a secret band of mercenaries, and the dice was rolled. Behind the shadows of her dark chamber, Chandralekha could hear the demons conspire. She didn't know how to douse Phalgun's manic obsession, but she was sure that her father would not stoop so low—or would he?

KshemGupt once again saw the tiger pouncing on him in his dreams and expressed his desire for hunting. Narvahan tried to persuade KshemGupt to focus on the kingdom as he had heard whispers of kings from neighbouring Himalayan kingdoms and Udhampur who had agreed to support Damars if they chose to revolt. KshemGupt, however, was in no mood to listen. He had even stopped caring for his favourite preys—the jackals. It was now tigers he was after.

'I need to put an end to this battle; the tiger and the sanyasi must die—I want no more dreams.'

Narvahan could sense the gloom inside KshemGupt. He knew KshemGupt was a brave man, but he was hollow from within. He never let anyone delve deep into his thoughts. Something was ailing him, and even Narvahan, being his confidant, couldn't get a finger on it. Why was the king hunting tigers? Where did that thought come from? It was a bad omen to hunt tigers in Kashmir as they were the symbols of 'Shakti',

Birth of the Queen and the Prophecy 13

the source of power for Lord Shiva, who was the presiding deity of Kashmir. Narvahan advised KshemGupt against the expedition, but he had made up his mind. Narvahan trembled with fear as he saw the hunting party depart. He ran towards the Padmaswamin temple just outside the capital city. 'Please stop this madness, please stop the curse from unfolding,' he begged at the feet of the Lord himself. But, could the wheel of time be stopped?

Sun had begun to delve over the western horizon by the time the hunting party reached deep into the dense forests of Pir Panjal Range. KrishnaGanga was KshemGupt's favourite resting spot. Legend had it that Lord Vishnu did not want the *asurs* (demons) to be partakers of the amrit—the nectar of immortality—that had come out after the Sagar Manthan in order to save the world. Despite all the devs guarding it, an asur, named Rahu, quietly infiltrated the devs and a drop of Amrit went into his mouth. Before anyone could react, Lord Vishnu cut-off his head, giving birth to Ketu—the headless one. Then, Lord Brahma brought the amrit kalash to KrishnaGanga and ordered Devi Sharda to sit atop it to protect it. Going forth, the place where Devi Sharda sat was revered as the Sharda temple. About 4,900 years ago, the temple complex came to be formally known as Sharda Vidyapeeth—the greatest seat of learning the gamut of Shakti Upasana. It became the world's first ever institution that offered degrees, diplomas, certificate courses and workshops in Tantra. Sharda Vidyapeeth would attract students from all over the world, from the furthermost corner of the east and the west, to learn the Vedic way of life.

KshemGupt ordered his entourage to camp at KrishnaGanga and dismounted his horse to bathe in the stimulating waters of the holy confluence. His mother had raised him with the stories of Lord Vishnu and every time he visited KrishnaGanga, the memories of his mother would flash by. The death of his mother had rattled KshemGupt; she was the only one who loved him dearly. Her death had left a vacuum in his life and it drew him further away from his father, King ParvGupt. Disturbed by the memories of his parents, KshemGupt ordered the hunt to begin, despite the darkness that had begun to envelop the jungle.

Soon the hunting party set out to look for their game. The jungle was abuzz with the sounds of the creatures of the dark. Birds of many shapes created a flutter that echoed across the dense jungle of lofty deodars. More than the sounds, KshemGupt felt being watched by the shadows or was it destiny smiling at him as he kept venturing deep into the playground of time. They moved quietly amidst the sound of leaves crumbling beneath their feet when they heard playful moans. The guides raised their hands, a signal that the prey had been spotted. Behind a foliage of blueberries, the prying eyes of the guides discovered a pair of tigers mating. The hunting party surrounded the tigers and KshemGupt killed one of them while the other managed to escape deep into the forest. His hunting party warned him that it was not a good sign as the tigress would come back to avenge the death of her mate. KshemGupt mocked them and said that he will find the tigress and kill tigress too. He mounted his horse and rode away into the forest to hunt the her down. He soon lost his way and found himself surrounded by an unfamiliar group of soldiers who escorted the defiant king respectfully to their base. KshemGupt was welcomed by Valaga—a tall, dark and sturdy woman who took him inside the camp.

Birth of the Queen and the Prophecy   15

As he walked, he noticed another figure behind a curtain and heard a laughter that infuriated him. 'Don't you know it is treason to ambush your king? I will have your head on a spike for all to see,' said KshemGupt.

'Why don't you make yourself comfortable and then we can decide what best to do with our heads!' said the voice sardonically, with a hint of playfulness. She moved the curtain with her sword, prompting KshemGupt to reach for his. But, before he could do so, he found his hands being immobilized by a vice-like grip, strong enough to stop his hands yet feminine to the touch. KshemGupt turned to find Valaga towering over him.

'Swords are not needed here. We are your well-wishers and you are safe here in my kingdom,' said the face which was still hidden in the darkness.

'Your kingdom?' KshemGupt said with contempt. He wanted to say more but he found himself manacled as the face drew into the light. The two eyes shone bright and dazzled him with the sparkle of a million stars; the face was a near-perfect oval with luscious lips, a willowy neck and more, but it was hidden in the darkness. KshemGupt found himself enchanted and drawn; he moved towards her as a moth to fire, to see more. After a step or two, he couldn't go further but he tried, and with every step, he felt a sharp pain in his chest.

'It would be sad to have your head on a spike even before we could discuss what to do with our heads,' those luscious lips spoke breaking the trance as KshemGupt saw a sword holding him back.

'Who are you?' asked a helpless king, spellbound and hankering to see more.

'You are in the company of Didda, the princess of Lohar, and you have trespassed, we assume accidentally, into our kingdom,' Valaga's stern foreign accent echoed in his ears.

Didda was an extraordinarily beautiful girl and KshemGupt was instantly mesmerized by her. In his consequent interaction with her, KshemGupt realized that Didda was a rare combination of beauty and intellect. His urge to possess Didda was instant.

'You don't seem to handle trespasses well,' said an enamoured KshemGupt.

'We usually slit open the trespasses; you won't enjoy the mess,' Didda almost snapped back. KshemGupt felt weak in her presence. After a friendly flirtatious banter, camaraderie developed between Didda and KshemGupt. Eventually, his own soldiers traced him, and he left for Srinagaram.

Somehow, he had an astounding feeling that Didda would be able to give him an heir to the throne. Without thinking much, he sent his proposal to King SimhRaj of Lohar seeking Didda's hand in marriage.

SimhRaj seemed apprehensive as he was unsure if KshemGupt knew everything about Didda. Many princes had declined to marry her in the past. After deliberations with his family and well-wishers, King SimhRaj invited KshemGupt to Loharin to spend some time with them before solemnizing the proposal of marriage. KshemGupt accepted the invitation and decided to visit Loharin. After a grand welcome, he met Didda for the second time at her palace and was all the more convinced and charmed by her intelligence and wit. She invited him to their annual palace games where she would also be participating in all the events, including a sprint.

KshemGupt told Didda, 'I am absolutely mesmerized by your skills.' Didda quipped, 'You haven't seen enough yet.

Tomorrow, you will be dumbstruck with what you see,' and smiled.

The next day, KshemGupt and the royal family were upon the rampart of the palace looking at the line-up of veiled faces. KshemGupt searched to spot Didda amongst the participants.

As the race commenced, a face appeared with a cane in hand yelling with excitement. KshemGupt was utterly shocked and intrigued when he realized that it was none other than his Didda riding on Valaga's back, whipping and urging her to run faster, making everyone watching the race feel as if she was sitting on a chariot. KshemGupt was shocked, but it also brought a cruel smile on his face.

KshemGupt was in awe and rose to applaud when Didda won the race. He was dazed and amazed seeing this facet of Didda. However, the smile turned into disbelief when he saw she was disabled, that the princess limped. KshemGupt found himself in a deep dilemma—should he marry a crippled princess?

Meanwhile, Didda went on to perform more tasks, such as archery, sword-fighting and horse-riding, and excelled in each of them.

In the night, SimhRaj invited KshemGupt for dinner and expressed his pleasure at meeting him. SimhRaj told KshemGupt that he had seen him as a child and that he was happy to have met him after so many years. SimhRaj and KshemGupt discussed various things and talked about his father ParvGupt. After dinner, SimhRaj told him that Didda's disability was the reason he wanted KshemGupt to come and see her for himself, so he could take an informed decision.

'I see that destiny has played its part in having the two of you meet; if you both agree to the match, who am I to object! I had always wanted my daughter to be married into the Kashmir dynasty,' said SimhRaj as KshemGupt listened thoughtfully.

'I desperately wanted a girl child after the birth of my two sons. I knew that in the times ahead, I could get my daughter married to another prince, which would help me further secure my kingdom. To fulfil this dream, I performed a Putrakameshti Yagya with a unique abhishek (or consecration) for Mahadev to seek a daughter,' continued SimhRaj.

'Soon, on the day of Janmashtami, as dusk descended over Loharin, the queen's chamber was filled with an infant's cries... My princess had arrived. But, soon enough, the cries of the child were joined by that of the queen. My happiness was short-lived as I realized that the daughter, whom I had yearned for so much, was born disabled.'

SimhRaj spoke so beguilingly, slowly, unfolding the events as they had happened that KshemGupt was drawn into the story through a timeless abyss.

The Loharin Palace was enveloped in gloom. In the dead of that night, SimhRaj left the palace with his beautiful little girl in a basket and headed towards the banks of the holy river Vitasta. Amidst the frightening thunder, he closed his eyes and let the basket drift away. As he turned to leave, he felt something stopping him. The king turned around to see the basket was entangled in his clothes. In a sudden flash of lightning, SimhRaj saw his beautiful baby's eyes gazing at him; she wasn't crying.

SimhRaj then looked up to the sky and screamed in self-loathing agony, 'Oh Lord Shiva, why did you cheat me? You are making me murder my own child! Why?' The thunder and lightning continued as if the Lord, himself, was answering his questions, but SimhRaj was consumed by his pain and guilt and did not feel or understand anything else. However, he could not conjure the courage to leave his baby behind. He took her back to the palace.

The young princess grew up in a hostile environment. She was ridiculed by her cousins and other children. Didda would run to her father and mother for comfort but they would be dispassionate towards her and saw her as a liability. Didda soon realized that she was an unwanted child in the palace. She longed for the love of her parents and would cry alone looking at the love other children got from their families.

One day, while wandering in the palace, she came across a section where the soldiers practised combat. Her eyes were suddenly lit up with joy as she watched the soldiers training with swords and various weapons with valour. She started visiting the area regularly and tried to emulate the techniques she saw. Often, she would fall down and injure herself.

Meanwhile, the queen mother ordered Valaga to be Didda's chaperone. About 6 feet tall and a well-built woman of an African origin, Valaga's family had served SimhRaj in his conquest into Africa. After the death of her father, SimhRaj had taken the infant Valaga into his care and the Queen Shreelekha treated her as her own. Loyalty and valour were ingrained into Valaga since infancy, and in the future, she would repay the royal family many times over with her commitment.

Didda continued to visit the barracks discreetly with Valaga. Soon, Didda was discovered by VikramSen, the chief trainer of the soldiers. Even though he was amused to see the young princess so passionate about combat, he turned her away. However, he would soon realize that Didda was not just any other girl. Didda used to practise the art of sword fighting with Valaga every morning in the palace premises. She would fall because of her disabled leg, but she kept getting back up. Nothing deterred her from standing up strongly, despite being bruised. Often her wounds would bleed, but she never cried. A childhood of ridicule had made Didda strong enough to not show her pain. VikramSen would watch her from a distance. Didda had requested him to be her guru several times, but VikramSen had always laughed it off. There was no way VikramSen would teach a crippled princess. Didda continued her practice relentlessly until it was time for the wheel of destiny to turn yet again.

It was Navreh—the New Year—in Lohar and in the whole of the Vedic world. With the first light of the sun kissing the peaks of Pir Panjal, Valaga walked into Didda's chamber and woke her up. Valaga was carrying the traditional thaal, or a plate, comprising the first flowers of spring, a few grains of rice, some sandalwood paste, fresh curd, jaggery, a diya and the most important thing—the Vedic almanac. For centuries, the almanac was at the core of the Vedic rituals. It comprised of the annual calendar and complex astrological calculations, including the minutest details of calculating the movements in the solar system. The day-to-day activities of the Vedic world were governed by this almanac.

Didda wanted to sleep for some more time but Valaga adoringly patted her face.

'It is Navreh, Didda; come look at the thaal. The new year has started, and it is time for a change,' said Valaga.

'New Year? Time for a change? Valaga, are you serious? Time doesn't change for a cripple.' Didda said scornfully.

Valaga understood her pain. She sat beside her and held Didda in her arms.

'I have checked your Varshphal, Didda, and this year is the year of change for you. The year will test your determination, courage and valour in an arduous way.'

'You call that a change? Change for good?' Didda exclaimed.

'Get ready, princess; it is time—Maharaj and Maharani would be ready to leave for Sharda Peeth soon,' Valaga was stern this time.

The Lohar royal family had a tradition of an annual havan at the Sharda temple every year. This year too, the entire royal family was visiting the temple for this ritual. This was the same Sharda temple where Lord Brahma had hidden the amrit and the place which eventually became Sharda Vidyapeeth, the foremost seat of Vedic education. The peeth also enclaved a temple dedicated to Goddess Saraswati.

Didda didn't want to go, but she thought it was perhaps one of those rare occasions when her parents allowed her to come near them. The thought of being with her parents brought back joy on her face and shimmer in her almond-shaped eyes. She hastened to get ready.

The journey to Sharda Vidyapeeth and the temple of Godess Sharda was through KrishnaGanga basin; the temple was further nestled up in the not-so-dense forest. One could hear the Vedic hymns from miles before and the fragrance of Isband and KainthGan from the fires of the havan kunds of the Peeth filled the souls with divinity and a sense of peace. The entire area of KrishnaGanga was believed to be full of miracles. Born of the two rivulets, the KrishnaGanga basin was believed to cure the incurable of diseases due to the influence of the amrit kalash being hidden deep under the sanctum sanctorum of Devi Sharda's wooden idol.

Valaga took Didda for a bath in the freezing waters of KrishnaGanga and blessed her. It was so unusual, Didda hardly complained about the water being too cold. Didda enjoyed the fringes of the world around her. SimhRaj and the queen too bathed nearby, the water was especially warmed for them.

After the rituals inside the temple, it was time for the darshan of the Divine Mother Sharda. SimhRaj and the queen made the first offering of flowers and exited after the mandatory pradakshina of the idol. Didda and Valaga followed. Didda, however, was unable to take her eyes off the captivating eyes of the Devi. She seemed to be communicating something. This was the first time that Didda had felt something unusual in the temple; she found herself in presence of the Divine Mother.

'It's time for a change,' Valaga's words echoed in her mind. Didda stood in front of the idol for a while and then made her offering as an anxious Valaga looked on.

SimhRaj and his queen retired to rest in their tents and summoned Valaga. Before they left, the queen advised the children to stick together and not wander into the forest. However, Didda, along with her siblings, sneaked out of the tents and went to the nearby Ganesh Ghati. It was a small valley within a valley with a flat hillock overlooking the valley. It was not the flat face of the hillock that was imposing but the Swyambhu Ganesh idol on the face of the rock. It was believed that Lord Ganesh, himself, was the presiding priest at the sthapana of Devi Sharda's idol. He was so mesmerized by the Divine Mother that he chose to stay in KrishnaGanga, inside

Birth of the Queen and the Prophecy 23

the hillock, and thus emerged the naturally-formed portraiture of Lord Ganesha in the rock on the face of the hill which became popularly known as Ganesh Ghati.

The children went deeper into the adjoining forest without realizing that they were being followed by a shining pair of prying eyes hidden behind the thick foliage. Soon, Didda realized something was trailing them and her mind started racing. She had to do something. Sensing danger, she screamed for all to run up to the trees. No sooner than the children climbed the trees, a full-grown tiger appeared from the foliage. He stared at Didda without moving. Didda realized that the tiger was identifying its prey. She noticed a fiery flicker in the eyes of the beast and knew that it was going to attack her.

Didda realized that she didn't have a chance to save herself as she couldn't climb a tree. In that moment, she also saw that her younger brother was on the ground, hiding behind the tree in a state of shock. Didda slowly moved towards her brother, maintaining eye contact. She seemed to be playing with the tiger's mind, keeping him occupied. In that very moment, when she managed to hold her brother by his arm, the tiger roared ferociously intimidating Didda.

She realized that she may not be able to help her brother up to the safety of the tree or on the ground. Her mind was racing, and just then, she saw something on the ground that made her stronger. The tiger started moving slowly towards Didda and she knew that the portentous moment had arrived. She began to sweat profusely as she stood resolutely facing the mauler. The roar of the tiger had alerted the guards and VikramSen himself led from the front. He arrived when the tiger was just a few paces away. He quickly lowered his body and crouched with his eyes fixated on Didda. VikramSen was almost paralysed with horror seeing what was unfolding in front of his eyes. A supreme warrior himself, he reached for his sword and whipped it out from his scabbard—a sight that would have withered away his fiercest of enemies, but this was not the usual enemy. In a matter of seconds, many things happened simultaneously... The feral predator leapt at Didda who bent down and grabbed something from the ground; while VikramSen lunged towards the tiger, piercing his sword through its body. The blade struck, and the beast rolled over with a menacing growl. The soldiers who had just arrived froze seeing this magnificent sight. Ganesh Ghati shuddered with the guttural roars of the tiger, the cries of the children and the joyous screams of the soldiers.

The tiger lay on the ground motionless. In this melee, Didda said, 'You are slow', looking at VikramSen. He was stunned to hear the words as he gathered himself from the dreaded encounter that could have killed him. He immediately looked around to see who had dared to utter those words.

As he turned, he saw an unfazed Didda still standing there. She seemed to mock VikramSen. He couldn't believe what he had just heard from Didda. The soldiers took the children to safety and soon Valaga arrived and hugged Didda. She hurriedly inspected Didda for any injuries and was relieved to find her unharmed.

Then, as Valaga came to terms with the near-death event, her worry paved way for anger.

'Did I not ask you to remain in the tents?' hollered Valaga.

'You are slow,' Didda repeated nonchalantly, still looking at VikramSen without paying any attention to Valaga's outburst.

'What did you mean?' VikramSen asked Didda in an annoyed tone.

'I had him before you could,' Didda said precociously and smiled.

VikramSen was completely flummoxed. He could not believe what he had just heard from a young girl who herself was crippled and had no chance of saving herself from the beast. Valaga held Didda by her elbow and apologized to VikramSen on Didda's behalf before frisking her away. Didda continued to stare at VikramSen with a smirk on her face.

His thoughts were broken by a soldier who presented VikramSen his sword. VikramSen moved towards the tiger and realized that it was still alive. The tiger was writhing in pain and his jaws were wide open, displaying his fang-like teeth that could have ripped off a human body. VikramSen was stunned to see a wooden stem wedged inside the tiger's jaw. The entire sequence of events played in front of his eyes once more. He realized that just before his sword pierced the tiger, Didda had picked up the sharp branch from the ground and had thrust it into the tiger's mouth. VikramSen immediately turned towards Didda's tent. He did not know what to say, so, he asked her whether she was afraid of the ferocious animal.

Didda firmly replied, 'I was not fearful of the beast. I had already trapped the tiger by staring into its eyes and if it was not for your sword, I would have easily killed it with the sharp branch I had grabbed from the ground.' After a pause, she lamented, 'I do not know how to use a sword. I wish I did.' Her words exuded confidence like a true warrior.

'I had asked you many times, and I ask you again; teach me,' Didda said.

VikramSen enquired why she wanted to learn the art of combat and warfare? Didda quickly replied, 'To protect my brothers and cousins in adversities. I want to take up the responsibility of protecting them.' She was worried about them, especially after seeing what could have happened to her younger brother.

VikramSen was impressed but he was cautious not to let his excitement surface.

VikramSen said, 'Luck favoured you today, but you might not be this lucky every time.'

Didda agreed to this and said, 'I was lucky as I got a chance to prove that courage does not lie in the sword but in the heart and mind of the warrior. I only wish I could explain it better.' She hinted innocently at VikramSen for the times he had declined to accept her as his student for learning swordsmanship.

VikramSen had never encountered a student who had proved his mettle at such a young age. However, he felt Didda had elements of arrogance which was inappropriate for a true warrior. So, he said in a condescending tone, 'In spite of being so confident that you could have managed to trap and kill the tiger without my support, why do you wish to learn these combat skills from me?'

Didda politely replied, 'Guruji, your name is known everywhere. All the enemies of the Loharin are scared to attack because they fear you.'

He quickly intercepted her, 'But, you just questioned the same VikramSen.'

Didda responded sharply, 'No! I just tried to explain that this is an apt opportunity for you to train me to prove yourself right.'

Didda's bold answer impressed VikramSen. He realized that she was not only courageous but also aware of her strength and abilities. However, to test her determination to learn further, he looked at her legs and said, 'Any training and knowledge shared with you will be wasted. You will not get to use any of it as you will be married in the next two to four years. I cannot waste my time on you.'

'I am a girl and a cripple—is that the reason you don't want to teach me? That something might happen to me?' Didda was bitter and scathing this time.

'You can assume that,' VikramSen too was cautious with his words.

'Till now, all the students that you have trained were not crippled and were boys. You have just witnessed how you have wasted your time training them; they were all on top of the trees, scared. Try your luck training me and who knows history may remember this student for her achievements.' She kept up her vitriolic attack on VikramSen.

VikramSen was surprised at being challenged by such a young girl, yet he was happy because he knew that she was right. Didda said as she gazed at him, 'Like every teacher yearns for a remarkable student, every student, too, looks forward to an outstanding teacher. By fighting this battle and killing the animal, I have just proved my worth.' Her thoughts and understanding belied her tender age.

'You will want to run away in two days,' VikramSen too kept needling her.

'Why do you decide everything?' She seemed irked by VikamSen's pungent remarks.

'Do you know how to swim?' He further prodded.

'No,' Didda promptly responded, not knowing where all this talk was leading to.

VikramSen then turned away to leave. Didda was heartbroken again. She felt VikramSen would never teach her; he was just toying with her. VikramSen stopped at the entrance of the tent and said, 'The next day we return to Srinagaram,' before walking out.

Didda stood there, almost in a daze, still trying to get over the words of VikramSen. She couldn't believe that she had been accepted as a student by the revered warrior VikramSen.

'It's time for a change,' she recalled Valaga's words.

Two days later, as the sun was breaking the horizon across the eastern peaks, VikramSen stood at the banks looking at a crippled girl wondering if not for her courage, she might not have been alive. This was the day Didda's training had begun. He started by asking Didda to stand on only her right leg. She lost her balance numerous times, but VikramSen maintained his strict instructions.

Didda was scared of falling into the water; but every time she fell, she managed to regain her balance. This 'training' continued on the second and third day as well. Didda was extremely upset with VikramSen but obeyed him nonetheless. On the fourth day, when VikramSen asked her to stand on one leg, she realized that not only was she able to balance herself on her right leg, she could even move her body in the same position.

On the fifth day, Didda received the same instruction. Out of boredom, she looked around her standing on one leg. She noticed that many swans too stood in the water on one leg with their eyes closed and used their other leg to catch fish.

Didda started to replicate the same action and continued all day.

On the eighth day, Didda realized that she had not been using her crippled leg effectively all these years, but in these last few days of training, she was finally able to use both her legs.

She realized that now she was able to put both her legs to use, she could move it the way she wanted while maintaining her balance.

She could stand steadily on the rocky and slippery banks of the Vitasta. The ability in her legs added to her strength and she could sense the anguish she felt for VikramSen fade away.

However, VikramSen did not want her to slow down because of her new-found confidence. For the next eight days, he made her stand on a boat that was being rocked continuously sideways by three soldiers.

He did not let her go till she managed to maintain her balance on the unsteady boat.

Along with this, VikramSen would make her stand in the waters of the river and instruct her to hold on to a branch of the trees planted on the shore. Didda would almost hang from the trees, using one arm while resting the other. Very soon, this continuous practice started to strengthen her arms more.

Didda would continue to fight her boredom by jumping from one branch to another, hanging around like primates. She soon started to emulate all the moves of an acrobat and her body got more and more flexible.

VikramSen had expected the same from Didda. He knew that she would continue to work her way forward if she was guided properly.

VikramSen moved her to the third level of their training.

She had to practise climbing a mountain. This was a painful exercise for someone with a disability, but it also started to bring forth and strengthen determination.

Many a times, if she did not complete her climb in the stipulated time, she would be compelled to come down sliding. This painful and time-consuming practice started to drain Didda and she started losing hope. She felt that VikramSen was being too harsh on her and her anguish towards him started to build again.

She began to excuse herself very often since the rigours of training caused her frequent injuries. She was unable to understand the motive behind this practice.

When Didda did not come for their sessions, VikramSen neither called on Didda nor did he reprimand her. This led to an ego tussle between the guru and his disciple. While Didda gave up on the training, her mind continued to wage a war against VikramSen. She presumed that VikramSen had put her through this torture on purpose and it was his way of retribution for questioning him. Didda thought that this was his ploy of subjecting her to such an intense form of training, so that she would give up the idea of becoming a warrior.

The days went by without Didda attending her training, but she continued to be restless. She was not sure what was bothering her more—the fact that she had failed to complete the training or VikramSen's attitude towards her? She had gotten used to the training which was making it difficult for her to sit idle in the palace. She finally went back to the arena where VikramSen used to impart his training. Seeing her there, VikramSen neither expressed any happiness nor did he have any grievances. He just ignored her.

Birth of the Queen and the Prophecy 31

Didda was simmering with anger. However, she was left with no choice but to continue training with her guru, the brutal taskmaster VikramSen. There were times when Didda would be almost in tears but VikramSen would ignore her emotions and continue with his difficult sessions.

One day, he took all his students to a hilltop and asked them to practise a sword fight amongst themselves. Didda also accompanied them.

While the trainees were practising, one of them collided with her. The impact was such that she lost her balance and began rolling down the hill. In that moment, Didda instinctively saved herself using the skills VikramSen had made her practise during the early days of intense training. She was quick to realize her fault and wanted to make amends with her guru. 'How can I restart my conversation with VikramSen?' This was the big question that loomed large in her head.

From the very next day, Didda restarted her training diligently. She would practise sitting on her haunches, climbing the hill and then rolling down. VikramSen observed her from a distance but said nothing. During these solo sessions, Didda became aware that her kingdom was in a mountainous region surrounded by forests on all sides. She immediately realized that this type of training was best suited for such a terrain.

During her days of training, she conversed with River Vitasta like never before. While she stood on one leg, she observed everything about the river and its surrounding—its course, the speed of its water, the river banks, the flora and fauna, the direction of the wind at different times of the day and much more. Every time she hung herself from a branch, she would think of ways a tree could help her in those hours of need. She also thought of the mighty mountains. If the enemy was at the peak, she would have to remain hidden and move forth. She understood that rolling down the hill was better than walking down in unforeseen circumstances.

A week passed by. Everyday, Didda would come and stand quietly in front of VikramSen after her practice sessions. VikramSen knew she repented her behaviour and gradually accepted her way of apology. He then handed Didda a 15-kilogram sword with the instruction of always keeping it with herself. Didda thought that VikramSen would notice her hard work and finally go easy on her with the sessions, but to her surprise, the sessions were so tough and gruelling that she felt she might die. Knowing the blunder she had committed earlier, she chose not to interfere. She followed and trusted her guru's methodology, but with some piquant anger.

She managed to pick up the 15-kg sword but keeping it by her side throughout the day was becoming increasingly difficult for her. However, within the next two months, Didda managed to reconcile carrying the sword through the day. Then came a time when she got so accustomed to the sword that without it, she felt empty and incomplete.

After learning to keep the sword by her side, she commenced her horse-riding practice holding arrows and the sword. This was no mean feat for Didda.

VikramSen had instructed her that she would always have to mount the horse using her crippled leg. She was also instructed to stay at the farm with the horses so that she could understand them better. She was responsible for feeding them as well as looking after them. Her previous practice sessions continued as well. With so much to do now, Didda hardly realized when the day ended and the night began. If this was not enough, VikramSen also instructed her to practise meditation at night.

Didda was unable to comprehend why she was being made to do these things. It had been almost five months since she had started carrying the sword with her. She was eager to start practising with it, but it didn't seem likely that VikramSen was anywhere close to starting her training with the sword. Didda continued to reap both anger and respect for her trainer. If VikramSen would ask her to complete 100 rounds of running, she would complete 101. This one extra round was the result of her anger towards VikramSen, but he always remained unperturbed. Her own web of thoughts kept Didda occupied.

Didda was irked with VikramSen as he had asked her to practise meditation. She had a misconception that only the people who were engaged in religious activities practised meditation, unlike warriors like her. She was vehemently against this practice and even shared her thoughts with VikramSen who allowed her to discontinue it. He said, 'We shall start archery practise from tomorrow.'

Didda had to hold her sword in one hand and shoot arrows as well while riding the horse and then jump down and land on one leg which was a very tough task. In eight sessions of this training, it was only twice or thrice that Didda managed to aim correctly. More often than not, the noise around her disturbed her and she missed the target. Despite repeated efforts, she could not perform as expected and this upset her the most.

She was now beginning to lose her temper frequently and got irritated without any reason. VikramSen knew very well that she was drained because of her long and arduous training in the last few months which was also causing these mood swings. Any more from his side and she would collapse.

So, VikramSen gave her the responsibility of making the arrows. He did not make her go through intense physical practise sessions but instead taught her about different types of arrows—which arrow weighed how much, how far would they go, how each one of them worked for different targets, how could they be sharpened and kept intact. After learning this, she would practise all these techniques while VikramSen would meditate.

Initially, Didda looked at her guru meditating and found it extremely boring but over a period of time, she started to observe the peace on his face, which attracted her towards meditation.

She began to sit besides VikramSen and meditate; her body was no longer stressed.

Slowly, she found harmony. One day, VikramSen instructed her to pick the bow and arrow and start practising everything again.

Meditation helped Didda's ability to focus and aim. It also allayed her anger towards VikramSen.

During the course of her training, she would ask questions but VikramSen never responded to all of them. Instead, he would urge her to find her own answers. Along with meditation, they started the sword-fighting session that she was expectantly waiting for.

Meditation proved extremely useful during the practise of sword fighting as well, as one needed to remain focussed on the enemy with the weapon in one's hand. Even a small mistake could prove fatal. The training began taking its toll on her and she would be drained after these sessions. Didda would almost cry and want to give up, but VikramSen, her guru, would not give up on her. Just as a true jeweller knows the value of a diamond, only VikramSen knew Didda's potential. Slowly but steadily, the sword-fighting sessions increased Didda's stamina.

It was unlike VikramSen to personally teach a girl the art of warfare and combat and see her take the lead, but he had made an exception in Didda's case as he had heard his conscience. He had also spoken to BheemShah, Didda's grandfather about her training. It was he who had shared his thoughts about Didda's marriage with VikramSen and mentioned, 'I feel it's unlikely anyone would want to marry her, so Didda needs to find her purpose. Maybe, it is Mahadev's blessing in disguise that Didda wants to learn warfare.' When BheemShah shared it with VikramSen, it became VikramSen's prerogative to train Didda in this unique way.

His gut feeling said that Didda could become an excellent warrior and a leader. Even the princes did not have as much potential as Didda. No battle was won only with strength, one also needed intelligence, knowledge, agility and effective decision-making to win a war and Didda possessed it all.

From the beginning, VikramSen knew that Didda would get fatigued, but she would stay adamant and not stop until she became a successful and able warrior. The only thing missing was a purpose and VikramSen precisely gave her that.

One day, while he was selecting a few students for a special training, he did not select Didda. She felt bad that despite being one of his best students, she was left out. When confronted by Didda, VikramSen simply told her that she would not be able to perform. Didda took this as a challenge and insisted on being selected but VikramSen did not relent. He said that to learn this new art, she would have to leave the palace.

Didda wondered what was the challenge for which she was not considered competent enough? VikramSen told her that in order to learn this new skill, she would have to alter her diet, behaviour and thoughts. Didda, being adamant, insisted on knowing more and it was only then that VikramSen revealed that it was a skill to develop one's body through yoga and tantra and use each part as a weapon. He explained that with this skill, anyone could defeat their enemy even without a weapon in their hands. This 'Niyuddha Tantra' was understood and mastered only by a few.

The very thought of using one's body as a weapon fascinated Didda immensely. Her excitement was palpable, and she wanted to learn more about this technique, but VikramSen refused to share anything more. This further augured Didda's curiosity and passion to learn this new skill. She told her guru that there was nothing in this world that she could not do.

The moment she said this, she had successfully taken the first step towards this art of warfare since the first rule of Niyuddha was that 'everything is possible'. On her insistence, VikramSen asked for her complete devotion and dedication for this form of combat as his fees. Didda took a vow that day that going forth she would never complain or ask VikramSen the reason behind any task he would ask her to perform. Her only aim was to obey his instructions, even if it meant jumping into a vessel of boiling oil.

Complete devotion was a challenge for Didda because she had always reasoned and asked for explanations and logic behind every action. But, she went against her natural trait and devoted herself unconditionally to learning the art of Niyuddha. Her real

Birth of the Queen and the Prophecy 37

test had now started. Even a moment of mistrust in VikramSen would take her further away from her goal but she wanted to witness the miraculous art of using the body as a weapon.

Didda started living in caves along with VikramSen. She would get up at three in the morning and complete all the steps of Ashtang Yoga. After which she would engage in hard labour and practice with different body parts scientifically. To increase her core strength, she would take up different forms of exercise. She immersed herself completely in the training and left the caves only after becoming a Niyuddha warrior.

To prove her mettle, VikramSen invited his best warriors to fight her but Didda defeated them all. VikramSen was proud of his disciple. At the end of their sessions, VikramSen blessed Didda by sharing the Kaan Mantra with her.

'It is pertinent for a warrior to keep control on their mind and heart because they are required to take important decisions such as when to stop a war. Winning every battle is not necessary but understanding what is required and when is more critical. Whether we need a battle or not is an important question one needs to answer. If a solution can be reached through mutual discussions, then one should adapt such a route instead of waging a war every time. This saves a lot of energy and resources that may be otherwise invested in small battles. A calm and composed mind is the biggest asset of a warrior because it's only a peaceful mind which guides one to the correct path leading to victory.'

After hearing this Kaan Mantra, Didda assimilated her guru's words in her mind.

VikramSen knew that Didda could become the greatest warrior only if she could somehow balance on both her legs.

So, VikramSen created a special contraption for her foot. This device was all that she needed to bring out her true potential. Soon, her parents learnt about Didda's achievements and were baffled to see that the little girl, whom they had abandoned from their hearts, had turned into such a great warrior. SimhRaj was in deep thought at the turn of events. He wondered if this was a message from the gods. Eventually, SimhRaj made an announcement that astonished the entire Lohar. He called out to all the gallant warriors and announced that he would bequeath a part of Lohar to anyone who defeated Didda. He also believed that in doing so, he might be able to marry off Didda as well.

During the competition, SimhRaj and the queen were spellbound as was the rest of Lohar who watched the disabled and abandoned girl defeat one warrior after the other. However, there was much more left to the spectacle. Once again, SimhRaj rose to make an announcement but this one shocked every soul in the arena. The final combat was to be between VikramSen and Didda—the teacher and the disciple were locked in a battle of the Titans. The entire arena watched in awe and silence as the clangour of swords reverberated all around—and then for a brief moment, there was absolute silence. Everyone seemed to have frozen and then an enormous euphoria erupted that reached for the skies—Didda had defeated VikramSen. It was a proud moment for SimhRaj, but it was VikramSen who was the proudest of them all.

A thunderstorm was gathering across the Lohar skies. An unruly streak of lightning and the accompanying thunder broke KshemGupt's trance as he gasped for breath. For a moment, he thought that he had been in a bewildering dream. SimhRaj turned towards him, 'I have great regard for your late father ParvGupt. He was a great man and a friend. That is why, it was important for me to tell you this story. Now, since you know everything, I want you to think and let me know of your decision. If not as a father, then as a king, I would be more than happy to have Didda married to you.'

Soon after, SimhRaj retired for the night to his chamber leaving KshemGupt in deep thought. In the middle of the night, KshemGupt decided to leave for Kashmir. A terrible bewilderment had consumed him; his heart was pounding and his mind, galloping. He desperately wanted to reach Kashmir and discuss with his friend and counsel Narvahan.

Narvahan heard intently what seemed to him a fairy tale, but, in the end, he suggested KshemGupt to go ahead with the marriage. Like SimhRaj, he also felt that this alliance would convert the friendship of Lohar into a permanent bond for Kashmir, aiding the much-needed trade and commerce for the region. It would also bring in happiness and hope with a reason to celebrate in the current gloomy days of the kingdom.

KshemGupt was lost in thought, overlooking the kingdom from the rampart of his palace. He hoped that Didda would give a legitimate heir to the throne.

'Worst case scenario,' Narvahan added nonchalantly, 'she will just be another addition to your harem.'

2

The Curse of Vitasta and the Dark Prophecy

The Lohar royal court was abuzz with a mellowed frenzy. SimhRaj sat in a pensive mood on his throne as RajBhushan, his prime minister, and Queen Shreelekha apprehensively gazed at him. The lines on the royal forehead were still pronounced and his eyes meandered into a void. SimhRaj was hesitant to celebrate. This was not the first time that the royal family had apprehensions because of Didda's infirmity. SimhRaj had always prayed, cursed and even cried in solitude; he had even squealed in remorse at the gods, every time he had to face a refusal. His heart had borne much more than a father and a king of SimhRaj's stature should have had to inure. SimhRaj seemed caught in a realm as he saw his whole life flash by.

'My king, you need to decide as Narvahanji is waiting,' said RajBhushan, breaking the king's trance.

SimhRaj got up from his throne and so did everyone else. Narvahan hesitantly got up too. An unknown fear was pawing at him as SimhRaj walked out of the court followed by RajBhushan. Narvahan stood still, unsure of the protocol.

Queen Shreelekha stepped down from the throne and walked towards Narvahan.

'You must pardon the king, moments like this have left deep scars in our hearts,' the queen said.

Narvahan bowed in reverence before the queen, 'I can understand, Your Highness. It must be devastating for both of you, but now, I assure you, the princess will have the love of the entire kingdom and the king who eagerly awaits his bride,' said Narvahan humbly, measuring every word.

SimhRaj went straight to his Lord, the presiding deity of Lohar and the Universe. He looked straight at the Swyambhu Shivling and the celestial Neelmani, which weighed 6,000 tandulas, adorning his third eye (where one tandula was equivalent to one grain of rice). It was said to have powers beyond measure. An entire universe seemed to be trapped within the Neelmani that dazzled with the first ray of sunshine. Staring at the Neelmani was prohibited; only the High Priest, Shivendra, could serve the Shivling besides SimhRaj. Legend had it that Lord Krishna himself had presented the Neelmani to his nephew, Abhimanyu, when he was anointed the king of the entire northern territories.

'You know SimhRaj, it is prohibited to stare at the Neelmani unless you want to be eternally entranced by the Lord himself,' said Shivendra, in a manner only he could.

'What do I do, Kulguru? He continues to play games with me, toys with me, rips my heart apart...' SimhRaj said as he continued to stare at the Neelmani from the corner of his eye.

'You asked him for this; he has only given you what you wanted, and he continues to do so, SimhRaj. You have lived in doubt for twenty-five years; you have dared to question the bounty that the Lord has bestowed on you, and the manner in which he has; accept him as he accepts your ignorance,' said Shivendra in a voice that was unyielding even in the presence of the king.

'For how long are we going to pretend not to say a "yes", my king?' Queen Shreelekha announced her presence.

SimhRaj turned around, walked up to Shreelekha and embraced her.

'We have never been good parents to Didda; we have never thought about her. Now, I am scared that we just might scar her further,' said SimhRaj.

Shivendra walked up to the royal couple as they pulled away from their embrace.

'Let His will be done; at least, remember the prophecy,' Shivendra patted the king's shoulder reassuringly.

'Prophecy? Oh yes! I do remember it, but I don't believe it, and you know that I don't.'

'SimhRaj, you dare not doubt Dev Rishi Kashyap. He who broke the mountains to drain Satisar and created this very land with the blessings of Devi Uma herself; you doubt his word?' Shivendra raised his voice as he spoke since only he could.

'Send the word,' said the king, thus ending the impasse and bent down to touch the priest's feet.

'It's not me, SimhRaj; it's all Him,' Shivendra respectfully held the king by his shoulders and turned to face the shivling. The Neelmani was shining bright. Destiny had rolled its dice.

Seven moons hence, KshemGupt arrived in Loharin for an unusual wedding. The entire Lohar was invited to the wedding of the princess who they never felt was worthy of their affection. She was a mere spectacle for them.

While Valaga initially found it difficult to accept this match, she later reconciled with the wedding. Didda also gave Valaga the highest honour by treating her as her mother during the wedding. Valaga also felt an unusual allure deep in her heart, beyond what could be explained in words. Valaga believed her entrusted motherhood to be a will of god when she began to lactate.

Valaga was the happiest when she saw Didda. She was the only one who had seen Didda's agony closely and had been a witness to Didda's yearning for the love of her own family. Valaga still remembered the evening when King SimhRaj celebrated Didda's birth as that of the goddess. And, it was the same night when he shunned Didda upon realizing that she was crippled. Everyone spurned the baby because she was a disabled child, considered accursed. SimhRaj ordered everyone to stay away from her. No one except Valaga realized that the little soul craved love and attention.

Valaga's love and care made it impossible for Didda to live without her. When all the sisters were applying haldi, or turmeric—a tradition where turmeric paste is smeared on the bride's hands and legs—Didda recalled her childhood when they never let go any opportunity to humiliate her. However, Didda was happy as KshemGupt had accepted her, someone who had been rejected by the entire world. In spite of all her flaws, his acceptance made Didda develop a certain fondness for KshemGupt. During the pre-wedding rituals, her face was lit up with joy because she finally had someone in her life who would love her and who could rise against the world only for her.

There was happiness all over the kingdom. The brothers,

who until then had not even spoken to Didda, were happily engrossed in completing the various wedding chores.

The rituals to welcome KshemGupt had begun. Didda was dressed up as a bride and was performing Gauri pooja. Valaga was by her side assisting her. However, she was also eager to see the rituals being performed for KshemGupt.

Didda looked at Valaga and immediately understood what was going on in her mind. Since Didda's childhood, they both had stood for each other indubitably, so much so that if one wished for something, the other would sacrifice her life to fulfil it.

Didda whispered something to her maids who giggled and ran away to the palace where KshemGupt was staying.

The wedding was about to begin. One of the maids came back and started narrating everything that was happening outside to Valaga. One of them revealed that KshemGupt was looking resplendent and the grand way King SimhRaj and the queen welcomed him. The queen looked magnificent with the prayer vessel in her hand. Another chamber maid came and narrated how the two brothers had welcomed KshemGupt with the manglacharan ritual as a mark of respect.

King SimhRaj completed the rest of the rituals that comprised of Tilak, Kalava, Kalash Poojan, Guru Vandana, Gauri Ganesh Poojan, Darvdev Namaskar and Swastivacham.

Valaga was extremely pleased hearing all this. Finally, one of the chamber maids rushed in and gave the news that KshemGupt had completed all the rituals and now was waiting for his bride. She also added that he looked radiant with a tika.

As soon as the bride was called, Didda could feel her excitement. She prayed to Goddess Parvati and clambered

Valaga's hand as she started to walk towards the mandap, the place where the wedding ceremony was to take place.

Didda reached the wedding venue surrounded by her cousins and maids. She looked so captivating that it left KshemGupt spellbound.

Amidst the rituals of aasan, Manglacharan, Kalash Poojan, Ardhya and Madhupaak, KshemGupt wished that Didda would look at him just once, but she was too shy. She kept completing one ritual after the other with her head bowed down. KshemGupt was getting impatient. He wanted Didda to look at him just once. He found this chance during the garlanding ceremony. He suddenly said, 'You are not my Didda.' This comment made her look up at him and wonder why he said so. She was the same Didda. This moment of wonder became KshemGupt's favourite. One comment had moved such a brave warrior princess. He could see vulnerability on her face and he liked what he saw. He could also see the love for himself in Didda's eyes. To calm Didda's fears, KshemGupt jokingly added, 'You are not my sister after all. What do I call you?'

Didda laughed at KshemGupt's wit and sense of humour. At that moment, Valaga knew that her daughter would always be happy with this man. The rest of the ceremonies were also completed smoothly—Vivah Ghoshna, Manglashtak, Uphaar, Haldi Ceremony, Kanyadaan, Gaudaan, Guptdaan, Panigrahan, Sheela Rohan, Lajoham, Saptapadi, etc. While performing these rituals together, the love between Didda and KshemGupt started to blossom.

The pride in KshemGupt's voice as he made the wedding announcement filled Didda with pride. She felt her fondness for KshemGupt grow.

While the hymns were being sung, Didda overheard KshemGupt recite them in the perfect way. He seemed to have selected every present for Didda very carefully.

This was also the first time she was sitting so close to her father. She was moved when KshemGupt gave her a reassuring look that he was there for her. She felt a spiritual connect with KshemGupt as soon as the wedding was solemnized.

She now had no complaints from her father. KshemGupt and Didda completed their pheras (the ritual of circumambulating around the holy fire by the bride and groom) and were now one. The newlywed couple was extremely happy.

The moment of Didda's bidaai (the sendoff of the bride to the groom's home) was near. Her mother could not be seen anywhere. Both her brothers looked for their mother frantically while she had been sitting in her room alone, engulfed by sadness and regret for not being able to give her child the love she deserved. She had no advice to give her daughter because she had never known her enough. As soon as her sons saw their mother in the crestfallen state, they were concerned of what might have happened to make her feel like that on such a momentous occasion. She then shared her anguish with them. The brothers, who till now, seemed to be happily participating in the wedding festivities asked their mother, 'For whom are you crying, mother? Instead, you should be happy that we are getting rid of this curse. Finally, someone has agreed to marry her. If KshemGupt had not agreed, our father would have had to face the wrath in hell because of not being able to perform her Kanyadaan. Whatever has happened has happened for the best; our burden has almost been lifted. Let's bid farewell to this curse as soon as possible.'

The Curse of Vitasta and the Dark Prophecy 47

Even though the mother did not like what her sons had to say, she did not utter a word. As soon as the queen and her sons stepped out of her chamber, they spotted Didda who had come to seek blessings, from her mother. Didda, who was filled with happiness until now, felt all the joy leaving her. She was about to leave without seeking her mother's blessings, but Valaga stopped her. Didda bowed down to touch her mother's feet. The queen could feel Didda's tears moisten her feet. As soon as the mother raised her hand to bless Didda, she caught hold of Valaga's hands and left the room.

Grief loomed large on the faces of both the brothers, not because they had hurt Didda, but because she had overheard their conversation. They worried that she might create a scene. The mother, on the other hand, was drowned in sorrow.

Didda was standing on the threshold of the palace. She was about to depart from this house which was no longer her own. She held Valaga's hands tightly. Valaga was the only one who felt the throes of Didda's separation. She wailed like a mother and would not let go of Didda even though KshemGupt was waiting for her.

Just when Didda was leaving the palace, Valaga turned to SimhRaj and said, 'Your Majesty, I had promised to look after Didda all my life—from the day I was entrusted to take care of her, right from her childhood. So, now please grant me the permission to go with her.'

Didda stared at the king and for the first time in her life, she saw her father looking back at her. She could see his happiness. He allowed Valaga to go with her. Didda bowed to take his blessings and he put his hand on her head. Didda felt that she had received the greatest gift, which she had longed all her life—her father's blessing. Sounds of the shehnai lilted in the air as Didda bid adieu to her home which never was.

Queen Chandralekha and Rajmata stood at the gates of the palace to welcome the wedding procession. Chandralekha had heard about Didda's disability. She was certain that KshemGupt would get over her very soon, and she would be lying in some corner of the palace. But, as soon as she saw Didda, she was captivated by her beauty and poise despite her pronounced disability. Chandralekha's confidence sank.

'I trust you will do your duty properly and not give lame excuses like others,' Rajmata taunted Didda while performing the aarti and applying tilak.

Didda had heard the word lame all her life. It was who she was and she didn't flinch as expected by Chandralekha and Phalgun. Didda responded with a smile as she bowed to touch her mother-in-law's feet.

Rajmata stopped Didda from touching her feet and gave her a hard look, unsure of what her smile meant. Didda was unusual in her demeanour and Rajmata along with the Maharani Chandralekha seemed flummoxed. Chandralekha came forward as Rajmata handed over the aarti thaal to her. After the aarti, Chandralekha poured her share of vengeance.

She embraced Didda, holding her firmly by her arms, almost squeezing them, and whispered menacingly, 'I hope you will deliver a miracle or else I shall welcome you in the harem after nine months.'

'Why don't you take your sister to the chamber?' Phalgun intervened sensing the anger in the air. He realized how difficult it would have been for Chandralekha to welcome someone who could reduce her to a chambermaid if she produced the heir.

Didda found herself surrounded by malicious people, which was distressing. The walk towards her chamber was difficult and suffocating. She felt a rage building deep inside her.

She had borne the brunt of humiliation from her people of Lohar since childhood, but she found the subtle psychological humiliation in Kashmir very demeaning and hurtful since she had expected a warm welcome in the new kingdom being their queen. Didda was also not used to veiled, emotional attacks.

She felt like tearing up all the finery she wore but sensed someone watching her. She stopped and turned around. It was Valaga who immediately understood her turmoil and came forward to put her arms around her child. They walked to the chamber as directed by the maids hand in hand.

Soon, KshemGupt also walked into the chamber along with Narvahan.

'I hope you are comfortable, Didda. Let me introduce my friend and trusted minister Narvahan,' he said without waiting for Didda's reaction. She was perplexed with the unexpected introduction on her first night at the palace.

'I shall leave Narvahan with you so that he can introduce our great kingdom to you.'

KshemGupt then walked a few steps and stopped. 'I shall see you soon,' he said.

Didda wanted to stop him but hesitated.

Narvahan sensed Didda's discomfort and introduced himself, again. He told Didda, 'I understand what you are going through. Rest assured, it is not you, but the entire kingdom is in turmoil. I am not sure if this is the best time or the worst time for you to be the queen.'

Didda looked out the majestic balcony overlooking

Srinagaram. It looked enveloped in gloom and the air inside the chamber also gushed out like a glorious era gone by.

'Kashmir is going through a low phase primarily because of the wars that have cost the kingdom dearly. Even the armies have rebelled, and many able commanders have deserted us.'

Narvahan's eyes turned moist with every word that he used to describe the plight of Kashmir. Didda felt the pain in his speech and realized that Narvahan was indeed a son of the soil. Pain had taught Didda to read and understand the human character as she had seen it all herself. Didda closed her eyes to visualize the plight of the minister as Narvahan continued the tragic tale of a ravaged Kashmir.

After the rebellion by the army, the kingdom had resorted to hiring soldiers, who would change allegiance often and constantly rise up against the rule. The entire kingdom was in disarray and people were left at the mercy of corrupt officials and an unjust system.

He explained the history of the northern frontiers of India and told her that it was as old as the Mahabharata war. King Gonanda was ruling the major northern territories encompassing Kashmir at the time of this war. Eventually, the Karkota dynasty gave the northern territories its greatest ruler—Lalitaditya. Filled with an unquenchable thirst for conquest, he conquered many countries across Asia. The Punjab, Kannauj, Tibet, Ladhak, Badakshan, Iran, Bihar, Gauda (Bengal), Kalinga (Odisha), South India, Gujarat, Malwa, Marwar and Sindh were all invaded by him. It was he who finally broke the power of Arabs in Sindh. All these victories created a feeling of pride among the people across India. By the turn of the eighth century, King Lalitaditya had created a pan-India empire, where he ruled as far as Afghanistan and Sindh in the northwest, Assam in the northeast, Tibet in the north, the Vindhyas in the central west and Gujarat in the west.

Lalitaditya built a new city called Parihaaspur on the outskirts of Srinagaram, including his palace that was adorned by jewels from the KrishnaGanga. The celestial beauty of the finest blue sapphires created a mesmerizing ambience at the royal court. Lalitaditya built four main temples, including one for Lord Vishnu (Muktakeshva) where the emperor used 84,000 tolas of gold to make the enchanting idol of the lord. It was believed that the Lord himself appeared during the pranpratishta. In the temple of Parihaskesana, Lalitaditya used over 20,000 tolas of silver to cast the image of Parihaskesana. By then, the Buddhist influence in Kashmir was also on the rise. So, as a tribute to Lord Buddha, he ordered a statue to be cast in pure copper by his finest craftsmen. Lalitaditya was present at the ceremony the day the statue was lifted off the ground. It was the month of Magh and it had begun to rain. As the statue rose to the thundering skies, it disappeared momentarily into the clouds. The entire city stood spellbound as the sun cracked open the dense clouds and shone brightly from behind Lord Buddha who seemed to be towering above everything else in the city. Soon, in AD 760, Emperor Lalitaditya died ending his glorious reign of nearly 36 years 7 months and 11 days. With him gone, Parihaaspur lost its status as the capital. Srinagaram, the subsequent capital, was built along the banks of Vitasta by the kings that followed; however, they could not stop the glory of the kingdom from waning.

By AD 900, the great dynasty and once prosperous kingdom had lost its former glory. Kashmir was on the precipice of no return when King Shankar Varman descended on the throne.

The reign of Shankar Varman was considered as the gravest period that Kashmir had ever faced. Famines struck when floods receded, and administration was as depraved as the king.

People scavenged for food and began to rebel as Shankar Varman was the cruellest king that Kashmir had ever seen. The subjects were baying for his blood, but he continued to sit on the throne drunk with power and Soma. The entire kingdom was on the verge of disintegration. But, none of it made a difference to Shankar Varman. He sat there unconcerned, as if waiting for the universe to set in motion a chain of events that would alter history.

ParvGupt, the army commander of the Kashmir kingdom urged the king to end his tyranny, or at least, stop excessive taxation on his subjects in the wake of recurring famines and floods.

'I am the God of Kashmir and the taxes will stay,' responded the king.

Most of the council of ministers told ParvGupt that it was about time Kashmir had an able king.

ParvGupt, backed by the council of ministers, led a mutiny to salvage the kingdom from the debauched King Shankar Varman. On that fateful night of amawas, or the lunar phase of the new moon, ParvGupt rebelled and they took over the royal palace. A majority of soldiers in the palace surrendered and a handful of them who resisted were slaughtered. Before Shankar Varman could even react, he found ParvGupt's sword at his neck.

He was shoved into a boat that slowly waded through the waters of Vitasta. ParvGupt and his loyal soldiers grappled

Shanker Varman to a stone with a heavy iron chain. He was then quietly dragged to the deck of the boat. Looking at his inevitable death with almost closed eyes in the dark waters of Vitasta, the captured king suddenly turned towards ParvGupt and said, 'I am leaving, ParvGupt; but remember, my soul will be back to be revenged. Neither you nor your name shall be remembered; for your own blood shall devour peace from your life and kingdom.' With that, he himself took the plunge into Vitasta. Weighed down by the stone, he instantly drowned. His words, however, kept ringing in ParvaGupt's ears even as he was being crowned the new king of Kashmir.

It was a joyous day not because ParvGupt was crowned king but also because his wife gave birth to a beautiful boy. Kashmir had a new king and a prince on the same day. Invitations were sent to the neighbouring kingdoms for celebration—especially to SimhRaj who came with his queen and baby Didda. ParvGupt and SimhRaj were good friends and when they met, ParvGupt instantly noticed that something was bothering SimhRaj.

It was during this time that a sanyasi, believed to possess miraculous powers, appeared on the Char Chinari—a small floating island with four chinar trees—in the mystical Lake Satisar. The word spread and both the kings decided to meet the sanyasi—more than ParvGupt, it was SimhRaj who was eager for the meeting because of his daughter. Both the kings, along with Didda, and ParvGupt's young son, crossed the Lake Satisar in a boat to reach the small island to seek the sanyasi's blessings. While the young prince was fascinated by the smile of the baby girl, SimhRaj looked on to the mesmerizing waters of the lake. Several creatures and a variety of rainbow trout displayed their colours in the waters, which was so clear that

SimhRaj felt that he could almost touch the bottom. His thoughts were interrupted as the boat anchored. The sanyasi was in deep meditation and the kings waited for him to open his eyes. After a while, the Sanyasi opened his eyes and told King SimhRaj, 'Your daughter has been touched by the holy Vitasta. She will create a destiny of her own.'

Pleased by the sanyasi's words, King SimhRaj had just begun to say, 'But, my daughter is...' The sanyasi snapped at him and told them to leave the rest to fate. Both the kings bowed in reverence and turned to leave while the sanyasi closed his eyes again. Just when the boat was about to leave, the sanyasi opened his eyes and yelled, 'But King ParvGupt, it will be your daughter-in-law who will change the fortune of your kingdom and not your son...not your son...' The prediction shocked ParvGupt who was reminded of the curse of the dying King Shankar Varman. Disturbed by the events, ParvGupt ordered the boat to move on.

'...And then?' probed Didda.

Narvahan continued, 'King SimhRaj returned to Lohar soon and there was complete silence thereafter. King ParvGupt invited King SimhRaj many times, but he would always politely decline.'

After a small pause, Narvahan said, 'It appears that KshemGupt and your destiny are intertwined right from your birth. The kingdom is waiting for the prophecy to come true. However, KshemGupt doesn't believe in such baloney.'

'Do you believe in it?' Didda asked Narvahan. But he just smiled almost knowing what was in the offing. Narvahan said, 'Your Highness, more than the prophecy, you should worry about Phalgun. He has quelled many a rebellion and served the kingdom well. He even sought the marriage of his daughter with the king as a prize for his service. You might have met her, Queen Chandralekha…'

'That means, he knew of the prophecy,' Didda interrupted.

Narvahan was taken aback by her spontaneity. He said, 'Yes, Phalgun does know about the prophecy, but you must remember that Chandralekha is extremely beautifu…'

'More beautiful than I am?' Didda snapped again.

A puzzled Narvahan said, 'The king thinks so.'

Didda snapped yet again, 'What do you think?'

Narvahan, for the first time, looked at Didda and was overwhelmed, both, by her beauty and demeanour. He could almost hear his heart pounding. He felt the chill of the sweat dripping down his forehead; something unexpected was about to happen or so he felt. A battle had begun in the palace corridors.

Phalgun was committing a grave mistake of ignoring the new queen, Didda. He was unaware that the queen was proficient in fifty-two different skills. However, he had a first-hand experience to this within the first three days.

Didda realized that everyone obeyed Phalgun in the court while Chandralekha commanded the palace. She also noticed that both of them were trying to keep KshemGupt away from her. He was kept busy the whole day, and when he would finally reach the palace in the evening, he was intoxicated and in an inebriated state. Didda was getting restless to meet her husband and talk to him.

She wanted to explore the entire palace, but Chandralekha was trying her best to curb her freedom, and so was Phalgun. They did not realize that Didda was not a person who could be chained.

KshemGupt also longed to spend time with Didda, but Phalgun kept him engaged in conversations and exploited his weakness for alcohol.

The desperation on both the sides was similar but there seemed to be no way out.

Didda was stunning, both in beauty and intellect. She disguised herself as a needy woman and reached the court with the story about a lost husband. She told the king that she had come to seek help in looking for her husband who was lost in the jungle. She added that she was going to search for him but if the royal guards found him first, they should tell him to meet her at the same place in the jungle where they had first met.

No one else except KshemGupt identified his queen. He was also eagerly waiting to meet Didda and her shrewdness added to his admiration for her. He immediately left for the jungle. The jungle became their abode for days to come. When Phalgun and Chandralekha realized that they had been taken for a fool, they began to conjure dark plots. Chandralekha was fighting for her position in KshemGupt's life as well as the palace, while Phalgun clearly worried about the throne.

3

The Sorcerer, the Death and the Birth of the King

The word had spread across the kingdom that the queen, the mother to the would-be saviour, had arrived. Soon, a new love story unfurled and to the utter surprise of all, KshemGupt seemed completely under the spell of his new queen. The populace even started calling him by the name of 'Diddakshema'.

However, Didda's mind was not at rest. Chandralekha's words kept echoing in her mind, 'You will join the harem after nine months.' Didda had spent a lifetime in an environment of ridicule, where no one ever gave her love, respect or an opportunity. Now, when she had KshemGupt's love and the respect of the public, she didn't want to let it slip from her hands. She continuously reminded herself of King BhimaShah's words that Kashmir was a land of unexplored opportunity for Didda. She had the knowledge and the ability, having learnt all that the scholars had to teach. Trade, commerce, infrastructure, law, the art of war and politics—Didda was a proponent of them all. She knew that if this opportunity was lost, she had nowhere to go and nothing to look forward to.

KshemGupt loved Didda dearly, and, for some reason, he took to Didda like a fish takes to the water—they were inseparable. Didda too loved him back to such an extent that she became KshemGupt's addiction. The corridors of the palace were rife with gossip about their love and life. People would often wonder how was it that a cripple was satisfying KshemGupt's satyromania? KshemGupt was so deeply in love that he got coins minted which had 'Didda KshemGupt Deva' inscribed on them.

Destiny watched over as a debauched king's love grew for his disabled wife every day. It was quite rare to find a husband adding his wife's name to his own, and seeing this tore Phalgun as well as Chandralekha's hearts.

It had been a month and the palace was abuzz with gossip of another kind. People were eager to know if the new queen was pregnant yet. They believed the time was ripe for the prophecy to come true. Valaga and Didda were worried, as they knew the queen wasn't pregnant. Valaga also understood the predicament Didda was in. This non-pregnancy could dislodge all the wonderful things that had happened over the last few months in Didda's life, and perhaps, if she was not pregnant soon, they might even send her back to Lohar.

Valaga advised Didda that it was time to breach Chandralekha defence while she would figure out what else could be done.

Didda went to meet Chandralekha who was sitting in her chamber. Chandralekha was visibly drunk and saw Didda's image entering her chamber in a huge ornate mirror against the wall. Chandralekha breathed heavily and her eyebrows tweaked in anger as she saw the beautiful reflection of Didda's face adorned with jewels passing through the mirror. Chandralekha was fuelled by a sudden rage and threw her glass of alcohol at the mirror. The chambermaids were stunned and immediately started cleaning the floor strewn by the shattered glass.

Didda stood unperturbed, with an orchestrated calm and poise that added fuel to the fire that burnt Chandralekha's heart to coal.

'That was a good throw; you really love me a lot, Chandralekha ji,' said Didda.

'Rani ji!' Chandralekha snapped, 'Mind your feet; sorry, mind your foot. The shards could hurt you,' she added while trying to gain control over her ghastly demeanour.

'Shards are what I have walked on all my life. It is the smooth floor that vexes me,' quipped Didda.

Then, she added softly, 'Neither have I come here to displease or disparage you nor have I come to remind you of your lost place in the king's heart. I am here just as a woman who hopes to make a friend,' Didda was calm and blatantly direct as was her way.

Didda's calm demeanour was beginning to have a soothing effect on Chandralekha as well. Her breath began to calm down, and her eyebrows returned to be the beautiful arches that they were. Her eyes were tad moist, because of the alcohol, which added to her luscious beauty.

'The most beautiful eyes there ever will be,' Didda looked at Chandralekha's eyes. A coy smile wiped the remaining traces of anger from Chandralekha's face and she walked up to the ivory table wrapped in Hangul skin.

With a slight gesture of her hand, she signalled for the chambermaids to leave. Chandralekha poured Soma into two glasses.

'I have been mean, and I am sure you can understand why,' she said handing the glass to Didda.

Didda had never tasted Soma before and VikramSen had forbidden the use of intoxicants of any kind. It was essential for a true warrior to be a devout disciple for life. It had served her well and Didda wished to remain the unparalleled warrior that she was.

'Have it,' Chandralekha stood there as Didda seemed lost in her thoughts. Didda had to make a quick decision.

Should she turn down the Soma and remain a devout disciple, or should she take it to break new ground? Being a warrior was something that meant everything to her and the abstinence from intoxicants was a holy oath that could not be broken. Being a warrior was not a means to brutal power but more of a conduit to her father's love.

As a child, Didda had always wondered why she was deprived of the warmth, the snugness and the care of her parents' lap when every other child in the palace had it in full measures. When she saw her father happy in the company of VikramSen and other army commanders of Lohar, she thought that maybe it was because she wasn't a warrior; maybe that was why her father didn't love her. What other reason could be there for him to despise her so much?

'Didda, why don't you drink the Soma?'

Chandralekha had been holding out the glass just for a while but for Didda, who had been lost in her own thoughts, it seemed like an eternity. A glass of Soma had taken her on a journey of a lifetime.

'My apologies, Chandralekha ji! It has been quite a while since I have had a sip and I was hoping you would teach me

The Sorcerer, the Death and the Birth of the King 61

a thing or two about Soma.'

Didda said in such a charming manner that Chandralekha could not hold her laughter.

People like Didda rewrite their own destinies unlike people at the altar, hoping to be rescued.

Soon, laughter began echoing out of the queen's chamber as they began to talk like women and soon as friends. A new era was unfolding in the Srinagaram palace and the laughter of the queens travelled on the whispers of the guards across the city.

Was Kashmir on the way to its former glory? The prophecy of Kashyap Rishi couldn't be untrue, right?

Back in the chambers, the queens spoke of the palace and their king, their husband.

'Is the prince on his way?' Suddenly, Chandralekha broached the topic much to Didda's delight. Gossip had never been of any interest to Didda.

'Yes,' Didda lied with a straight face. 'That can't be true! He is cursed! He can't even sire a child, let alone an heir,' said Chandralekha, who was intoxicated enough to forget her surroundings.

Didda's mind was racing, yet she managed to keep her face devoid of expression. Her heart began to pound and Chandralekha's words seemed feeble. Sweltering profusely, Didda excused herself from the chamber. The entire world around her seemed to be reeling; she wasn't even sure if she would make it to her chamber.

Didda's mind was under duress and she heard whispers telling her what would happen if she would not give the kingdom an heir it longed for. Various permutations appeared before her—an unceremonious return to Lohar, sitting alone in a corner of the harem… These thoughts continued till she could stand no more. She gave up and allowed herself to fall. Valaga quickly held Didda in her arms and put her to rest on the majestic silk bed.

Next morning, Didda opened her eyes and hurriedly stood up, recollecting the events of the previous night that had brought back the uncertainty in her life. Valaga sat on the bed and held Didda in her reassuring arms. Just then, a chambermaid announced the arrival of Rajmata.

'We have seen almost thirty-two suns since you have come here and yet I see you in the dark, Didda,' said Rajmata. She had been constantly enquiring about Didda's status—it had been almost a month into their marriage and the entire kingdom was expecting good news.

Didda was extremely perturbed, while Chandralekha seemed to be getting the better hand out of the situation. She was certain of her return as the favoured queen once Rajmata announced that she would call the raj vaid to examine Didda the next day.

Didda became anxious after Rajmata's announcement and sought Valaga's advice. In these circumstances, Valaga was unable to guide her causing further mental agony to Didda. She locked herself in her chamber and shut herself from the world.

Narvahan was informed about the new developments. He immediately paid her a visit. Somehow, Didda knew Narvahan could be trusted and Valaga opened the chamber doors for him. As soon as Didda saw him, she exclaimed, 'It seems my luck is about to run out as I am not yet pregnant.'

'And you perhaps never will be,' Narvahan responded sharply.

Didda was flummoxed that Narvahan knew all along how things would turn out. Narvahan continued, 'Your Highness, I am aware that the excessive abuse of various intoxicants has taken a toll on King KshemGupt.'

'Narvahan ji, how could you do this to my daughter? It took her a lifetime to accept that finally, something good is happening for her. Moreover, now, having come thus far, you are saying that it was all for nothing? Do you even realize this would ruin my daughter's life forever?' Valaga snapped at Narvahan. He could see a mother's pain in Valaga. This was no ordinary situation for Narvahan as he was apparently lost in thought, seeking a solution for Didda.

Narvahan too had begun to like Didda, not just because she was his friend's consort, but also he had begun to respect her as a woman. It appeared impossible to not be affected by Didda's charisma and Narvahan was no exception. All of a sudden, as if struck by an epiphany, Narvahan became cheerful and started snapping his fingers in excitement. Both Valaga and Didda looked up at him in confusion.

'AbhinavGupt,' said Narvahan.

'AbhinavGupt?' repeated Didda.

'Narvahan ji, do you really think he would help me? Why then has he not helped Chandralekha? After all, she too could have requested him and perhaps ordered him as the queen of Kashmir. Even the king himself could have asked him. AbhinavGupt would never say no to the king, or would he?' Didda looked at Narvahan with hope gleaming in her eyes.

'Yes, he could say no to Chandralekha and even to the king. There was no one who could make him do things against his will. Even Phalgun had tried but they all have failed,' said Narvahan.

'Tried and failed? Then, I will surely try.'

Didda rose from her seat as if she had found her lost vigour. She rushed to Narvahan, held him by his arm and asked him to be taken to AbhinavGupt. Narvahan was amazed at her exuberance and innocence.

Narvahan told Didda, 'One cannot just walk into AbhinavGupt's hermitage without a prior protocol. Let us not do what Phalgun and Chandralekha have done and been at the receiving end of his wrath.'

Didda understood what Narvahan was trying to say. AbhinavGupt was no ordinary being. But, Valaga had no clue about AbhinavGupt. She was still not able to understand how he could make the impossible, possible.

Puzzled by Narvahan's statements, she asked, 'Who is this AbhinavGupt, and how come he can help in all this?'

Narvahan was visibly surprised, 'You are asking me to tell you who AbhinavGupt is. Well, his greatness is such that no words can describe it.'

Didda explained, 'He is one of the greatest saints born on this land. He is a yogi. He is a yoginibhu, one born out of the womb of the yogini herself. A blessing of the Bhairava, he was born with exceptional spiritual and intellectual powers.'

'But, how can he help us?' enquired Valaga.

'He has acquired great abilities because of his devotion and meditation for years. He is one of the greatest followers of the Kaula. Not one, but more than fifteen gurus have graced him with their knowledge and powers,' Narvahan eulogized.

Didda then spoke, 'He has attained spiritual liberation through his Kaula practice under the guidance of his most admired master, Sambhunatha. Sambhunatha taught him the fourth school (Ardha-Trayambaka). This school is, in fact, Kaula, and it was emanated from Trayambaka's daughter. He has attained the eight great powers of siddhi, encompassing Anima—the power to assimilate oneself with an atom; Mahima—the power to expand oneself into space; Laghima—the power to be as light as a strand of cotton; Garima—the power to be as heavy as the heaviest thing in the universe; Prapti—the power to travel anywhere in this universe; Prakamya—the power to grant and fulfil all desires and wishes; Ishvata—power to create anything; Vasvita—the power to command all.'

Narvahan and Valaga listened without batting an eyelid. They were in awe of AbhinavGupt as well as of Didda's remarkable knowledge. 'That is not all,' Didda continued, 'Not just siddhis, but he also exhibits the six illustrious spiritual signs.'

'Spiritual signs?'

'Unwavering devotion to Shiva; attainment of mantra siddhi; control over the five elements; capacity to accomplish anything; complete knowledge and command over all arts and science; and the spontaneous attainment of all philosophical knowledge.'

Didda seemed oblivious to her surroundings as she spoke about AbhinavGupt. With dilated eyes, looking into the nothingness of space and time, she seemed to be drawn spontaneously to AbhinavGupt and his deific aura.

Hearing about AbhinavGupt, Valaga was convinced that Narvahan had suggested them the right path. 'But how will you reach out to him?' Valaga asked Didda, gently nudging her.

'Venom with venom, darkness with darkness and knowledge with knowledge,' Didda replied. She was in control of her thoughts and Valaga realized Didda had a plan.

'Shastrarth!' said Didda.

Narvahan exclaimed, 'Are you in your senses? How can you challenge the man of such vast knowledge, spiritual attainment and power? Even if you do dare to do so, you might strangle all your hopes with your own hands.'

'I know, Narvahan ji, it is not easy, but this is the only way left. I will try my best,' replied Didda.

Narvahan sent a message to AbhinavGupt that Queen Didda would like to meet him in Shastrarth. Having assimilated the knowledge of fourteen pre-eminent gurus of the world, AbhinavGupt's desire to seek knowledge was not still assuaged. He, too, thirsted for more. He readily accepted the challenge and called Didda for a meeting.

Narvahan was relieved as AbhinavGupt had at least accepted Didda's request to meet her. AbhinavGupt was amazed by her charm and courage to challenge him. When they met, he said, 'Answer three simple questions; if you answer them correctly, only then I will consider you capable of a shastrarth.'

'I am ready, Your Holiness.'

AbhinavGupt asked his first question, 'What is life?'

'The struggle and journey to attain moksha,' Didda replied.

He asked his second question, 'Who attains moksha?'

'One who gets to know himself and meets his atma attains moksha.'

And then, his final question, 'How will one know himself?'

Didda replied, 'Free yourself from desires, break the chain of karma and karm-phal.'

AbhinavGupt was impressed, 'I am moved by your wisdom Didda. I know you have come here for a purpose. You have proved yourself worthy and I cannot further engage in Shastrartha with you. I bless you that for whatever reason you have come here for, may Lord Shiva take care of it.'

This was exactly what Didda wanted. She beamed and bowed to take the blessings of AbhinavGupt. They, then, returned to the palace, content.

In the meantime, Raj Vaid Sushen had arrived in the palace to examine Didda. When he emerged out of the room along with Rajmata, Chandralekha and Phalgun were waiting outside presuming that Didda's supremacy was about to come to an end. The raj vaid seemed perplexed. Something was amiss and he was lightly stroking his long beard. Phalgun walked up to him and asked for his opinion. He had a vicious smile across his face as if anticipating a long dark night was about to be disseminated.

When the raj vaid announced that Didda was indeed pregnant, Chandralekha and Phalgun felt the ground beneath their feet tremble. Rajmata's joy knew no bounds as she took off a necklace she was wearing and handed it over to the raj vaid. Almost dancing on her feet, she ordered the servants to bring in sweets and distribute them in the kingdom. The news blazoned like fire as the kingdom of Kashmir had an heir.

'Light diyas of ghee everywhere in the palace; let it bathe in a new light as Kashmir is going to get its heir,' Rajmata instructed Chandralekha. At that moment, Phalgun saw the throne slip from his grasp. His lifelong dream of ascension to Kashmir's throne disappeared before his eyes. Chandralekha could not stop the tears from rolling down her cheeks either. Humiliated, she began to sniffle and ran towards her chamber.

When KshemGupt got the news, he too was elated with joy. He rushed to Didda's room, hugged her and promised that he would give her everything she desired for what she had done for him and his kingdom.

Soon, Didda became the beloved of Rajmata, and KshemGupt was in seventh heaven—after all, Didda had fulfilled his dream. Rajmata made special arrangements to comfort her daughter-in-law. She herself took care of her every need thereafter. KshemGupt ordered that the queen would not be left alone for even a moment; five-six attendants were to be present at her disposal at all times. Her chamber was beautifully decorated and adorned with paintings of Lord Shiva and Lord Krishna. The raj pandit was requested to visit her daily to recite the Vedas, Upnishads and other stories that would have a virtuous effect on the prince in her womb. Day by day, their love for Didda increased.

The whole kingdom celebrated the *godh bharai* ceremony, or baby shower, of the young queen. The palace was lit up with colourful diyas and everyone from the kingdom was invited for the feast. Everyone had been waiting for this moment. It had finally arrived and soon the kingdom of Kashmir would have its saviour. Rajmata made special preparations for the occasion. She invited saints and priests from different kingdoms to bestow their blessings on her daughter-in-law. She donated ten thousand cows and took a vow of performing a Mahayajna on the birth of their heir.

Everyone in the palace danced to the beat of the mridangam. Musicians played beautiful raagas and women sang traditional songs welcoming the child. Amidst the celebrations, KshemGupt was constantly looking with admiration at Didda. Finally, he found the right moment to compliment her. He held Didda's hand and asked her if she needed anything. Didda kept her other hand on his and said, 'You have already given me so much love and happiness, My Lord. What else can I ask for, but there is one thing I wish I could get for our people.'

'Of course, Didda, I will give you anything you want.'

'I wish that now you will take the concerns of the subjects more seriously. A king is only because of his people. I want you to be their ideal king, as generous as Lord Ram and as just as Vikramaditya.'

'Do not worry, Didda, leave the matters of the kingdom to me and you just take care of that boy inside you.'

'I am sorry if I said something wrong but believe me, I only meant good for the kingdom and especially you, My Lord. If you cannot promise me this, then at least allow me to visit the kingdom sometimes so that I can be there with them in their joys and sorrows.'

'God has been really kind, Didda, that he gave me you. Despite having a child in your womb, you have not forgotten your people. I appreciate your ability to be a mother and a queen at the same time. I promise I will not stop you in this.'

The king made his promise. She got what she wanted. However, Didda wasn't at peace. She was continuously thinking; her mind was racing all the time. Deep inside, she knew she couldn't leave things to chance. Didda needed a grip on the kingdom. Soon, she visited various parts of the kingdom, with Narvahan as her guide.

One day, when she went around one of the cities, she saw that the whole city was desolate. No one greeted her. No one chanted her name. When she enquired about the reason behind the city's deserted look, she learnt that one of the king's old soldiers had become a robber. He called himself Durjan.

He and his men looted people, molested women and killed anybody who tried to stop them. He was so dangerous that not even the king's men were able to catch him.

Didda called Narvahan and said, 'Write on the city square that if Durjan comes again, it would be the last day of his life. It's a promise of the queen to her people.'

'But, my queen, you don't know how fierce that man can be. I think you should reconsider your decision. Let me handle this matter,' replied Narvahan. But, Didda refused to change her mind and the notice was put on the city square.

Durjan took the challenge by a woman, even the queen, as an insult. As soon as he heard this, with his bunch of hooligans, he entered the city the very next evening. Didda was already waiting for him with Narvahan and her troops.

A battle began between Didda and Durjan. He was defeated and taken into custody to be presented before the king. The kingdom reverberated with chants of 'Rani Didda ki jai'. The people were now free from the fear and the brutality of Durjan.

The women of the capital came to Didda to thank her. They gathered around her and wanted to get just one glimpse of the queen who had become their saviour and inspiration. The kingdom started respecting their queen even more. She became their goddess who had all the qualities of Goddess Durga. They believed that their beloved Goddess Parvati herself had come to earth in Didda's form, possessing her qualities of beauty, courage and wisdom. Didda engaged with the people and ensured instant justice, often by beheading the guilty.

The fear was so intense that even the officials started to shiver at the very mention of Didda. Eventually, the enmity reached a crescendo and many attempts were made, not just

The Sorcerer, the Death and the Birth of the King 71

on her life, but on KshemGupt's as well. She survived and saved the king with her foresight and wisdom.

Phalgun, on the other hand, was deeply perturbed. He realized that, eventually, Didda might make him completely redundant. Phalgun confronted KshemGupt along with major ministers and made him see that what Didda had been doing was unacceptable. The delegation convinced the king that Didda's actions were humiliating the ministers and soon no one would respect them.

KshemGupt, who had always been easy to sway, was enraged with Didda and ordered her not to interfere in the matters of public administration. He wanted Didda to focus on the welfare of their future heir. Narvahan waited for the right opportunity and convinced KshemGupt to go out of the palace on a tour of the capital in disguise. It was the first time in years that the king toured his capital, mostly because he had never heard a good thing about himself or his rule. Somehow, he knew that his people did not respect him as a king.

KshemGupt was flabbergasted when he heard what people had to say about him. His eyes gleamed with pride—for the first time since becoming king. KshemGupt heard people praise his rule and remark on how Didda brought this welcome change. They mentioned that Didda not only ruled the heart of her husband but also the hearts of the people.

Didda's influence, however, created rivalries and enmities for her, especially that of the well-entrenched Prime Minister Phalgun. However, the prime minister had decided that he would not give up easily.

One day, Chandralekha asked him, 'What will we do now, father?' To her surprise, Phalgun replied, 'Nothing! I can do nothing. Didda has turned the game in her favour. Now, with these rounds of the kingdom, she has come even closer to KshemGupt. This is our fate, daughter. We have to live with this and accept that now it's not you who rules the heart of our king. Didda is the real queen and we should start treating her like one. I think it's time to seek her apology for all that we have done to her. Let's take some sweets and apologize to her and the king as well.'

Chandralekha could not believe that her father had lost so easily but accepted his decision and agreed to go with him to apologize to Didda.

When Phalgun and Chandralekha reached Didda's chamber, they saw that Didda was sitting with KshemGupt, who was carefully massaging her belly. When he saw them coming, he straightened himself and asked, 'Now what complaint of Didda has brought you here, Phalgun? What's so serious that you cannot wait to see me in the court?'

'I am sorry, My Lord. I have come with no complaints, but indeed, I wanted to apologize for all that I have done earlier. My love for my daughter had blinded me, and I could not accept Didda taking her place. I never respected her; I did not even bless her for her child. I always wanted to draw your attention back to my daughter for which I now plead guilty. I have realized how kind and generous our Queen Didda is. She is the most beautiful and has the courage to take care of the kingdom and be your queen. It was my mistake I treated her this way.'

He suddenly fell at KshemGupt's feet and lamented, 'My king, I have come here to ask for forgiveness from you and the queen. I understand that Didda is just like Chandralekha. I know now that I have been blessed with another daughter.

The Sorcerer, the Death and the Birth of the King 73

Please grace me with forgiveness and allow me to congratulate you both for giving us the precious gift of the heir to our beloved kingdom. I have brought some sweets for the two of you. Kindly accept these, so that we can make a new beginning.'

As the king approached to take a sweet, Didda felt something was wrong. She moved forward and enacted to stumble upon Phalgun, tossing the sweets out of his hands.

'I am sorry, My Lord, I think my leg got stuck in the carpet,' she said with a smile.

Phalgun was frustrated; Didda had, once again, washed off all his plans. He walked out of the room in disgust.

Chandralekha could not understand anything, 'Father, you went in with such a humble note, what made you so angry suddenly?'

'That Didda, she is the reason for all my pain. How well I had planned to make the king and Didda fall into my trap. Had they eaten the sweets, the poison would have killed them. Then, there would have been nobody between the crown and me. However, that Didda has outplayed me once again. I will not let her be.'

Phalgun attempted to kill Didda and the child in her womb multiple times, but she saved herself every time with her exceptional alertness and presence of mind. Not only did she wreck all of Phalgun's plans, but also kept gaining more respect in the eyes of KshemGupt.

When the news arrived that the Queen Didda had given birth to a son, the entire kingdom erupted with joy. Didda had fulfilled her promise and the biggest dream of KshemGupt—his legitimate heir had arrived. Both Kashmir and the shahi kingdoms were suffused with royal celebrations. One lakh horses and a thousand elephants were brought from across various kingdoms to help in the arrangements. Royal families from all the neighbouring kingdoms were invited. Popular delicacies from different parts of the kingdom were ordered for the feast. The kingdom was decorated with special flowers from different parts of the world. Water from the seven sacred rivers of the north, southwest and east were brought for the holy bath of the queen. On the day of the celebration, she was weighed against gold that was distributed amongst her subjects. All reverent priests were invited to bless the mother and the son. AbhinavGupt was specially invited who came to bless the newborn. Artists, dancers and singers were called from all around the world to perform in the royal court to celebrate the birth of their prince. One thousand and eight kunds were created to perform the Mahayagna. SimhRaj and the proud grandfather, the powerful BheemShah, visited Kashmir to see the newborn.

SimhRaj and Shreelekha were deeply moved to see the glory of their daughter. Upon seeing his grandson, SimhRaj recalled that night in Loharin when he was about to kill his daughter. Both the parents embraced Didda and they cried for a long time. The tears from the parents mixed with those of Didda and washed away the traces of the suppressed anger that she had held in her heart for years. Motherhood had added a new dimension to Didda's character.

The shahi king built the Bhimakeshava temple near Martanda to celebrate the birth of the prince and named him Abhimanyu in the memory of the great warrior Abhimanyu— son of Arjun.

Was it destiny or a cruel coincidence that the prince was

named Abhimanyu for he would usher in another poignant phase in the Kashmir dynasty and in the life of his mother? Destiny had not yet finished crafting Didda's life.

However, life had a different plan for Didda. While she had immersed herself in the upbringing of the prince, life took another turn. KshemGupt felt an urge to hunt again as he hadn't done so in many years. The young Abhimanyu and Didda both against the idea but somehow, he just felt he needed to go, and with his hunting party, he set out for the alpine jungles of the north.

Time turned and all of a sudden, an enormous tigress appeared on the scene and pounced on the king. Everyone was in shock; they weren't in a position to kill the huge beast. KshemGupt fought the tiger alone and it took a while before he killed it. The king was severely wounded, and his condition deteriorated rapidly. He was taken to the Kshemamatha in Varahamula just about 50 km west of Srinagaram in the care of royal physicians. But the king's condition deteriorated further. The royal guards then sent a messenger to the queen to inform her of the situation.

Didda rushed with Narvahan to Kshemamatha where the king was being treated. The few steps inside the camp were the heaviest she had ever walked. She left her son Abhimanyu and walked inside stoically to see KshemGupt who was breathing his last. Those few steps would usher in a whole new destiny full of excruciating trials.

Having seen her husband grievously wounded, Didda felt an unbearable pain tearing her heart. Withering in pain, KshemGupt looked at Didda and a feeble smile appeared on his face. He stared at her as Didda struggled to sit beside him.

She didn't know how to react; she wondered if her pain was greater than that of her king. She felt an uncontrollable urge to scream as the only man who ever loved her lay in a pool of blood.

KshemGupt had never known Didda as someone who would wilt. In those moments, he saw all his years with her flash by in a blur—his chanced meeting with Didda, the time they spent in Lohrin, their wedding and everything else that had happened in those last few years. In Didda, he saw the best years of his life.

KshemGupt attempted to reach out to Didda but he could not, and his hand dropped midway. Didda's heart sank further into an abyss of pain as she saw a part of his flesh missing on his arm. Didda's face was blank, she clenched her teeth as strongly as she could, but her eyes welled up, and tears rolled down her face. In those moments, she realized KshemGupt was breathing his last. In a matter of seconds, she would lose everything God had just given her.

Didda reached out to KshemGupt and gently placed her hand on his. Her hand shook, and her body trembled as she felt his warm blood. Narvahan couldn't hold himself outside much longer. He decided to walk in with Abhimanyu. In spite of being a man of strong heart, Narvahan found the sight unbearable and embraced little Abhimanyu.

'You can't save me?' KshemGupt spoke in a feeble voice. It was not a statement but a question, Didda realized soon after.

She could hold her cries no more and bear no longer. She felt the extreme pangs of losing her husband reach a crescendo inside her. Didda turned her head up towards her Lord, clenched her fists and screamed. She had never cried before, she did not even know how to cry but this time, she wailed.

'You can't save me,' KshemGupt spoke again. This time it was not a question.

'I have to go now, Didda,' said the king as he looked into her eyes, those beautiful almond-shaped eyes fighting the bravest battle.

He held Didda's hand again and said that he knew of his incompetence as a king. Perhaps, he wasn't made to be a king, but in Didda, he saw all the qualities that a ruler must possess.

'It is my last wish and my final order, and dear Narvahan will bear witness to this. Didda will be the custodian of the throne of Kashmir and ensure that only an able ruler must rule. Till the time Abhimanyu is not worthy, she should ensure that the integrity of the kingdom is maintained. Many internal enemies have harmed Kashmir and she must remain cautious and train Abhimanyu to be a valiant and just king. And, if he doesn't prove to be a worthy king, don't let him... Didda don't let him rule.'

'Don't do this to me. I am but just a girl and I need you...' Didda said with her eyes still closed as tears rolled down her face.

'Don't do this,' she repeated softly.

There was a deafening silence as KshemGupt did not respond.

'Please,' Didda trembled with fear, wishing away what had happened. The next part of her destiny had cruelly, yet silently, rolled over. SangramDev's curse seemed to have been fulfilled.

Narvahan, himself grief-stricken, tried to console the queen and the prince.

4

The Battle of Pattan and the Practice of Sati

Narvahan announced about the demise of the king to the royal guard. He also informed them that KshemGupt had appointed Didda as the regent and Abhimanyu as the king. Soon, all of them set out to return to the capital with the body of KshemGupt.

There existed a few black sheep amongst the faithful guards and the word reached Prime Minister Phalgun. The sadness of losing the king, his son-in-law, soon paved way to a cruel gleam in his eyes. 'Had fate made it possible for him?' he wondered with a sudden childlike exuberance. His heart was pounding as he began to visualize the mist clearing from the throne that seemed to have disappeared with Didda's arrival in Kashmir.

Phalgun paced across his chamber and waited for his trusted aide, Chandrabhan, who had arrived with his pack. These cunning men spoke in the shadows of deceit—hatching plans of death, spewing venom and consumed with nothing but the lust for the throne.

Chandrabhan bowed and left. His orders were clear—no survivours. Phalgun sunk into a chair trying to control his heartbeat. He was sweating as his mind raced along with the murderous pack of men galloping through the banks of Vitasta towards their target. His chain of thought was interrupted by the touch of Kashmiri silk on his forehead. He could not see clearly as his vision was still blurred with that of power.

'Chandralekha!' he exclaimed as he identified the scent of her scarf.

'What are you doing? Why have you become a murderer?' It was Chandralekha indeed.

'Can't you see? It's fate, it's written in the stars—this is my last chance. Gods have given me this opportunity, you know. I didn't wish for the king to die, did I?' he said with extreme compassion in his voice and tears in his eyes. A baffled Chandralekha looked at her father and all she could see was the lunacy of a man consumed with power.

'You shall be a real queen soon, my darling,' Phalgun whispered, oblivious of the pain in Chandralekha's eyes.

The wind was sombre across the meadows of Pattan, whispering into Didda's ear as she rode towards Srinagaram with her husband's dead body and young Abhimanyu in her arms. Didda was unaware of the message carried by the winds that deals had been struck, conspiracies hatched, and murderous plans had already been set afoot. Didda could barely suppress her grief and with every step towards the palace, she wondered about her life and the fate of the young prince. In just a few hours, she found herself at the crossroads of life once again, something she had almost forgotten with the love that KshemGupt showered on her.

In the last eight years, she had forgotten the regrettable life at Lohar and her disability. With just one uncouth stroke, destiny had snatched away everything that she believed was hers. With a million storms raging inside her, Didda continued her journey unaware of the heinous battle that had begun for the throne.

Soldiers' chatter broke her thoughts and Didda raised her head. Some of the soldiers informed her of the incoming troops, perhaps, from Srinagaram. Didda was sure that the word would have reached the palace and they would be waiting for their king. But, the calm of the dark night was broken by cries of men and the clanging of swords. Didda was unsure of what she heard. She grew anxious as she saw Valaga gallop towards her. It was an ambush and her soldiers fell one after the other, failing against what seemed battle-hardened mercenaries. Didda was stunned for she had never expected an attack at such a time. She was in a stupor. Valaga shook her and screamed at her, 'Didda, save yourself, save Abhimanyu!' Valaga shouted again and again. The very mention of Abhimanyu broke her daze. Swiftly, she gathered herself and handed Abhimanyu to Valaga. She realized this was a battle for the throne and the orders would have been to kill them all. Suddenly, she saw an enemy soldier riding towards Valaga; she knew Abhimanyu would be slaughtered if she didn't do anything.

VikramSen's teachings resonated in her mind. She reached for the sword and bawled loudly, temporarily halting the soldier in his tracks. Didda rode towards him and the soldier was caught unprepared as Didda's sword cut across his chest. Other soldiers were taken aback at the felling of their soldier. Their orders were to kill a helpless, grieving widow who was disabled along with her young child. With just one piercing scream that echoed across the dead of the night and the gale of her sword, Didda had managed to halt the marauders for a while. But it wasn't over yet. Didda knew that the soldiers would compose themselves and attack again any moment. It was in those brief moments when Didda realized that all the skills taught by VikramSen were about to be put to an ultimate test. She recalled what VikramSen always said, 'Everyone can learn to be a soldier, but the true merit of a soldier is in implementing his skills in an extremely adverse situation.'

Didda had trained for such times; this was her first true war.

As she rode towards the pack of men, still unsure of their plan, Didda swooped down upon them, clobbering them one after the other. She rose like thunder and descended like a tornado on the mercenaries. Didda continued slicing through them and her sword sung with her in unison. The remaining loyal soldiers were awestruck. Their crippled queen was in an avatar beyond their imagination.

They were shocked as they watched the 'ranchandi roop' of Didda. Abhimanyu was so scared that he hid in the arms of Valaga who bellowed with pride. In just a few hours, all of them had forgotten about the death of their king; it was a battle for redemption and a disabled woman transformed into a warrior. Didda found her true calling, under the merciless eyes of her destiny.

There were just five survivours when they resumed their arduous journey back to the kingdom, led by the queen. In the dark of the night, her faithful guards briefed her on the continued threat to her life and that of the young prince.

They told her that the kingdom and many of its courtiers truly mourned the great loss they had suffered, but a few wanted to take advantage of the situation. The throne was vacant again and they thought that they had a chance to claim it.

However, there was one hurdle in their way which could take everything away from them—Didda. Phalgun was the only one who controlled the strings. He plotted, schemed and manipulated weak men to support him. He knew he had to get rid of Didda to fulfil his ambition of becoming the king and he knew that that was the only time he would ever have the chance.

Phalgun, along with his allies, tried to create a wave against Didda amongst the other courtiers. He prevailed upon them that the legacy of their great kingdom should not go into the hands of a disabled woman, 'If she returned to the palace, she would try to take over the throne and we would all be left powerless in the court. She would bring in new people and appoint her men from Lohrin for significant positions. The throne deserves better than Didda. Let's stop her before she brings any misfortune on us, or on our kingdom.'

On her way back, Didda continued to feel the ruthlessness of her loss. She was perplexed, and different thoughts assailed her mind. She had lost the only man who had loved her despite her disability. In this moment of turmoil, a great challenge faced her. KshemGupt had given her the responsibility to look after the kingdom. She wanted to cry aloud but had to keep calm in front of her troops. She had to stay strong. Abhimanyu, Kashmir, the crown and an endless struggle with enemies, she had a lot of things to manage.

Phalgun had expected the turn of events—the loss of the mercenaries. This was the reason he had tried to convince the court against Didda and had succeeded. When Didda reached the palace, members of the court, led by Phalgun, stopped her and Narvahan, at the gates. However, the subjects, who were waiting for their king and Didda, were enraged by this act.

'We will not let you enter the palace,' said one of the ministers.

'You are a bad omen for the kingdom. You came into the king's life as a curse. We will not let the kingdom suffer anymore because of you. Go away, this palace has no place for the likes of you,' another minister added.

'You are right, dear ministers. This woman loved neither the king nor the kingdom. She only loved the throne and the power that came with it. This is the only reason why she has come back,' Phalgun said, adding fuel to the fire. This enraged the courtiers who suddenly pulled out their swords and stepped forward to attack her.

Bereaved and grief-stricken Didda implored, 'Stop! Wait! What is wrong with all of you? Don't you have any shame? In this time of agony, how can you be concerned about power? Don't you have any respect left for your king? You are not even letting his body inside? Does your king deserve this? Is this the way you will bid farewell to His Majesty? The king will curse you from heaven above for treating him and his queen in this manner. Mark my words, your deeds today will leave you suffering tomorrow. And then you will not be able to do anything but just regret.'

The ministers were taken aback by her words. They retreated and Phalgun realized that Didda had beaten him again without as much as lifting a finger.

'Well, if you want to enter, rest assured, you will be meeting your death,' said Phalgun.

'How dare you threaten the queen? My sword will slit

your throat for this, Phalgun,' Narvahan lashed out.

'You may cut my neck for sure but that would not save Didda from following the tradition.'

'What tradition?'

'Sati. Every queen must sacrifice herself in the funeral pyre of her husband and so will Didda. If you manage to enter the palace, you shall not be spared from this tradition.'

'How can Didda perform sati? The king has made her the custodian of the crown. She has promised him that she will take care of his kingdom.'

'Even the king is bound by customs and traditions. It's for her to decide if she wants to leave the kingdom with her son and end all the claims she had on the king or the throne or enter the palace and follow the custom.'

'I accept. I will perform sati. But you must assure me that once I enter the palace, you will take care of the promise I made to my lord. You will take care of my son Abhimanyu till he becomes eligible to become the king. You will look after him as your grandson,' Didda urged seeking a promise from Phalgun.

Phalgun realized that this was his golden chance. The hurdle would go away by itself. There would be no problems after Didda. Her son was too young to worry about.

'My dream has come true. I shall finally be the king.' Phalgun smiled inwardly.

'I assure you, Didda. The king's last words are of prime importance to me. I will make sure that your son grows up well and becomes an able king,' replied Phalgun.

'Don't get emotional, my queen. Let not sentiments take over your senses. You cannot perform sati. You cannot die. You cannot leave us. The future of Kashmir lies in your hands,

Didda. Please think again,' Narvahan said, perturbed.

'I have thought about it, Narvahan. If this is the custom, I will stand by it,' Didda told Narvahan and entered the palace.

Preparations were on for the funeral to be held the following day. That night was the most terrible night of her life. The palace haunted her. There was a deep sense of insecurity in her heart. Without KshemGupt, the palace seemed desolate.

The next morning, the pyre was set for KshemGupt's funeral. It seemed like the whole kingdom had gathered in the capital to catch a last glimpse of their king. The air was filled with the cries of the people of Kashmir, for they mourned the loss of their beloved king... The king who had just begun to be liked by his subjects and had recently given them moments of joy by marrying Didda but had suddenly left them with a huge vacuous pain.

The time had come. The priest asked Abhimanyu to come forward and light his father's pyre. Little Abhimanyu walked up with Narvahan. The priest gave him the kalash. Abhimanyu unaware of what was going on, looked around for his mother who was nowhere to be seen. He began to cry in fear. Narvahan held his hand and helped him complete the parikrama, or circumambulation around the pyre.

With each step Abhimanyu took, the crowd wailed louder. Everyone was in tears except Phalgun, whose eyes lit brightly with a cruel gleam. The people cried their hearts out for the young prince. Watching him, so young and in the grips of grief and fear, gave them horripilation.

'He was born to bear the onus of the whole kingdom on his little shoulders. Who would have thought that he would bear the burden of his father's body at such a young age?'

'What poor destiny has the lord created to this child? He has been orphaned so early, even before knowing the meaning of the term.'

'Hope that God keeps him safe from all the trouble and he is as good as his mother when he graces the throne,' the crowd muttered.

Then came the moment when the priest ordered the royal fleet to fire arrows in the air in respect for their king. Every swordsman had his sword down as a tribute when the funeral pyre was lit.

Now was the time for the queen to perform sati. Being the first queen of King KshemGupt, Chandralekha had to perform sati first.

She knew that it was her father, driven by his greed, who had led her to this end. Still, she held a profound belief that her father would not let her die. He would save her from the infernal fire; it was just one of his ploys to get rid of Didda. He would never let her die.

Chandralekha kept thinking all this as she approached the pyre. She slowed down as she came closer and looked into the eyes of her father with desperation. She remembered the time from her childhood when he had risked his life to save her when some rival ministers set their house on fire. She recalled he had once promised to give her everything she desired. He had her betrothed and married to the king, made her the queen and had tried everything to make her retain her position.

'I love you, father; you have saved me all my life. Do something now please. Save me again from this plight.' Her eyes seemed to cry out to Phalgun. Phalgun's eyes, however, reflected only his covetousness. The love had yielded to his avarice. He only wanted the throne. His daughter could not help him get it, but her death will surely do.

The father within him cried, but the diplomat inside him wallowed in the victory. Even though tears trickled down his face, but the look in his eyes made Chandralekha realize that all the love her father had professed for her was, after all, fake. He had just used her as a pawn to find his way to the throne. She was shattered to see such deceit, her love for her father vanished in an instant. Her father whom she had considered her saviour turned out to be her nemesis. She had nothing left to live for and leapt into the flames of the pyre.

It was now Didda's turn to perform sati. As she started approaching the pyre, the crowd shouted to stop her. Narvahan also implored her to stop. Women from the capital broke down the barricades and ran towards their queen to meet her for the last time. They lamented this cruel tradition and questioned the fate of women. They even tried to come close to her and stop her. The queen had been a pioneer, a trailblazer and an innovator. She could change this custom too. They called out to her but were pushed back by Phalgun's men.

Didda stopped near the pyre and turned around.

She said, 'I know it's a custom. But customs are made for people, by them, not the other way round. People come first, and it is evident that people need me more than the custom. I decide here that I will not give up my life in this way. I will not perform sati. I have promised the king to look after our son and take care of the kingdom and I shall do so.'

To which Phalgun replied, 'But you also promised to commit sati. And, as I said, worry not for your son. I will take the best care of him.'

'You being a father could not prevent your own daughter from dying in front of your eyes, how can you ever protect my son?'

Phalgun realized that Didda had deftly vanquished him again. He did not know what to do, what to say. With one successful manoeuvre, Didda had once more wiped off his dream. Phalgun drew his sword and ordered his men to kill the traitorous Didda. The perpetrators and loyalists once again clashed, the palace was covered in the blood of men who were merely pawns in the hands of two extraordinary minds. Narvahan sent Didda and Abhimanyu away to safety and took charge against Phalgun. By dawn, Phalgun realized he had no option but to retreat and he fled the palace with his remaining men. The funeral processions were over and Didda took over the reins of the kingdom as a guardian and a regent.

5

The Temple Siege and the Rise of the Ekangi's

Didda's tact for politics, negotiations and strategy were at work. She subverted grave conspiracies hatched to kill her and the young prince.

One day, in the dead of the night, her royal faithful guards stormed into her chambers and informed her that a wing of the palace and a part of the city had been set on fire. They also told her that a few men, loyal to Phalgun, might have plotted her murder. That night, Didda realized that she would always have to be prepared for war and there stood a risk of losing her life along with her young son. She soon appointed new ministers and henchmen to support her in the administration of the kingdom. Narvahan was appointed as the new prime minister and commander-in-chief of the Kashmir army.

Didda became suspicious of everyone. Meanwhile, she started training her son to become the next king. Her sole objective was to fulfil her promise to KshemGupt. She wanted to renounce materialistic life as soon as Abhimanyu was ready for the throne. Soon, her fears began to take shape as she faced her first direct challenge.

On her visit to Padmaswamin temple, located in the outskirts of the kingdom, an army organized by her own relatives had surrounded her.

It was Didda's first tryst with treachery as she saw KshemGupt's sister's sons, Mahiman and Patala, leading the siege. They had gathered allies who were largely Brahmin armies from Lalitadityapur.

She whisked away her son to a math, or hermitage, where Brahmin priests lived with some of her royal guards, and then began to negotiate with her relations. During these negotiations, she managed to bribe some of the supporters and placate the others. The situation was resolved.

Phalgun had fled to the northeast after Queen Didda ousted him from the kingdom. He had lost everything. He could not reconcile to the fact that he had been defeated by a woman, and that too a disabled one, who was younger than he was—both in age and experience. The fact that she was also a close ally of AbhinavGupt added to his fear and anxiety.

However, Phalgun didn't stay put even after the defeat and he conspired against Didda once again from outskirts of the kingdom.

The two nephews of KshemGupt—Mahiman and Patala—started living within the palace walls. Gradually, Phalgun built his relationships with both of them. He met them covertly and sowed the seeds of dispute in their minds by convincing them that they could be the potential successors to the throne.

Mahiman and Patala found a political ally in a Turk named Himmaka, and together, they started planning a coup against Didda. Didda, on the other hand, had already seen the imminent danger and expelled both of them from the kingdom. Mahiman and Patala found refuge under the rule of their father-in-law, King Shaktisen. Even though Didda had warned Shaktisen of taking any steps against her, he did not pay heed.

However, Mahiman conspired and persuaded people that any kingdom ruled by a woman, child or a wasteful king would ultimately fall. He tried to convince the people that if Didda were not removed from the throne, the Muslim invaders would destroy the entire kingdom. The Brahmins began to believe him and people gradually started to raise their voices against their queen.

One day, the queen went to offer her respects to Devi Padmaswamin. Her five-year-old son, Abhimanyu, Narvahan and about fifty soldiers accompanied her. The queen had no idea that death lurked around the corner. A temple was the last place anyone could think of orchestrating an attack. Weapons were not allowed inside the temples, so Narvahan chose to wait near Gopur. However, as soon as the queen entered the temple, she sensed danger. She noticed the body language of a few worshippers inside the temple premises. They seemed too disciplined to be commoners, and instead of worshiping the Goddess, they seemed alert and observant. The queen, without raising suspicion, quietly looked around and realized that there were at least 500 men inside the temple premises waiting to attack her.

She also realized that only Phalgun could plot something like this against her. She returned to Narvahan and looked at her small group of fifty soldiers; she knew that this was not the best time to attack her enemies. It could be a dangerous decision. Narvahan looked at the queen and understood what was on her mind.

She said loudly for everyone to hear, 'Narvahan has served the kingdom for all these years. His sword has always protected this kingdom. I want to offer prayers to the goddess for the safety of this kingdom along with this sword. I want to place this sword in the hands of my son so that in times to come, he grows up to be as courageous as Nirvahan.' She took Narvahan's sword, picked up her son and walked towards the temple premises.

Didda was shrewd enough to identify the leader of these rebels surrounding her. She could clearly identify the leader who had been keeping vigil on his men and their respective positions.

The moment Narvahan saw the queen enter the temple, he ordered one of his soldiers to be by her side. The rebel leader was relieved to see Narvahan unarmed. The queen noticed the expression of relief on his face and was sure he was the leader.

She continued to walk inside the temple and on reaching the main temple area; she saw that it was the usual priest. However, he was devoid of the usual warmth and respect. It did not take much time for the queen to realize that the priest was also a part of the conspiracy. However, she kept her calm. The queen, along with her son, Abhimanyu, completed the aarti. The priest also worshipped her sword and she offered prasad (offering) to the goddess. Didda slowly positioned herself close to the priest in such a manner that only he could hear what she spoke.

It was a tradition to offer dakshina, or donation, to the priest in return for the prayers he offered to the goddess on behalf of the devotee. The queen asked the priest, 'What will you accept as dakshina to let go of my son's life?' The priest was taken aback. His face turned pale. The queen told him that she knew what was about to happen in the temple premises. She added that she would leave her son inside the main temple area and go out to complete her prayer parikrama.

Didda also told the priest in an arresting voice, 'Shut the main temple area and do not open it till further orders from me. Keep my son safe and I will bestow enough gold on you to fill your house. But, if you side with the rebels, I will not forgive you.'

The queen further added, 'I am leaving my son to you so you can decide whether you want to save yourself from the sin of killing a child or be a part of it.' The priest was cornered and was left with no alternative but to obey the queen.

Didda instructed her son to stay inside at all costs and went out to complete her parikrama, as a mother determined to save her son. The queen, who always circumambulated the temple thrice, announced that she would undertake 108 parikramas to seek special blessings for her son. She started the parikramas as if she was weaving a web of protection around her son inside the Garbh Griha. The rebel leader and his army had no choice but to wait for the queen to complete her prayers and come out.

Didda, however, was just bidding for time so that her army would reach her. She knew very well that without it she could not attack her enemies. Therefore, she continued her parikramas slowly with a pronounced limp. Tension and anxiety lingered in the air. The rebels were ready to attack but could not do anything until the queen was in the temple curtilage. They had to wait for her to come out and their restlessness continued to grow.

Suddenly, Didda noticed Mahiman and Patala enter the temple. Their grim countenance told Didda that they were here with the intention to kill the little prince. With no successor, Didda would have to step down as the queen. Didda felt bilious when she saw her son's enemies but quickly regained her composure. She wanted to keep a safe distance between them and her son; she started walking towards them.

Didda was a Niyuddha—skilled in the art of combat without weapons and had trained to conjoin body and mind as a lethal weapon. She, thus, started a conversation with her nephews to portray that everything was all right between them.

'Welcome, Mahiman and Patala. What a coincidence! I was looking for you and as fate would have it, you are here in the temple, seems like God is very kind to me. I can't tell how pleased I am to see you. I would like to apologize to you for I have realized that turning you away from the kingdom was a mistake. After all, how could I manage to rule a kingdom all by myself? Especially after what Phalgun did, I can only trust my own people,' Didda said, hiding her derision.

On hearing this, Patala and Mahiman were left muddled. They were not sure if they could believe the queen. Didda, on her part, didn't mean the things she said she was only interested in keeping them occupied in a conversation. Just then, she noticed the Himank approaching with his warriors. They surrounded the temple and Himank entered the complex to speak to Mahiman and Patala. 'If the Queen needs your help in running the kingdom, offer her your help but what is the need to leave the prince alive? If you spare his life today, you will never become the king. You may or may not get another chance like this to kill the prince; so kill him now. If you want, I will also take away this queen of yours,' said Himank.

Himank's words prompted a measured smile across Didda's

face. She instantly realized that Himank's words would anger everyone, even the rebel leaders because how can someone talk about 'taking their queen away'. Didda saw this question on everyone's face. But, Narvahan, in his rage, started to walk towards the Turk king and was easily captured. The queen also noticed that Mahiman and Patala had readily agreed to the Turk's proposition and had begun to move towards the main temple area to kill the prince. She needed more time as her army was still not around. Didda quickly went up to Himank and said, 'Please wait, at least allow me to see my son once.' Himank was an ardent admirer of Didda's beauty and could not refuse her.

Didda quickly proceeded towards the Garbh Griha. She stopped suddenly, turned to Himank and said, 'This kingdom and its people have given so much to me, now is the time that I want to give something back to them. Please allow me to do so.'

'What do you want to give back?' asked Himank.

Didda was covered in fine jewelry. She looked at them and said, 'I have only these to offer.' She looked around and said, 'If today I was in the palace, I would have left so much for everyone present here but at this moment I only have my jewelry to offer. God willing, I would offer more in future.'

She took all her jewels and walked up to Himank and handed them to him and said, 'Mahiman and Patala did not even think once before handing over their own uncle's wife to a Turk, if they become the kings tomorrow, think of what will happen to your wives. I am going to take back my sword kept in the shrine while you think whose side you are on—mine or theirs?'

Didda was oozing confidence. She knew she had rolled

a winner. She went in, picked up her sword and hinted the priest to shut the door of the Garbh Griha. She then came out in the open, challenging an army of 500 soldiers like a true warrior. She was ready to fight all of them alone. Till now, they only knew of a crippled woman named Didda; now they were about to see a lethal warrior, ready to wage a war by herself.

It was a battle like never before, a pack of fifty, led by a tigress, tore through the Turkish army. Narvahan, on the other hand, fought Mahiman and Patala. Didda's incredible valour prompted the rebels to switch sides. Soon enough, the temple compound was flushed with blood and bodies lay strewn around. History had never witnessed a blood bath and treachery of this magnitude inside the sacred walls of a temple. Didda's valour must have prompted even the gods to pick a side. Didda won much more than a battle that day. Himank was vanquished and decapitated at the altar of the Divine Mother. They captured and imprisoned Mahiman and Patala.

The Padmaswamin encounter left a deep and lasting impact on Queen Didda and led to her radical transformation. She realized that such people like Mahiman and Patala needed to be crushed or else she would end up living a fearful life forever in a disordered kingdom.

The political chaos took a toll on Didda. She grew extremely lonely and weary of people because of their betrayal. She felt that her childhood had returned to haunt her. Didda knew she was unwanted and that men around her detested her. Powerful nobles and kings never wanted to accept that a woman could be a better administrator. In such times of loneliness, there was no one who understood that she never wanted the kingdom or to be the queen.

The Temple Siege and the Rise of the Ekangi's 97

The recent events at the Padmaswamin temple had been tormenting her mind. The need to have personal bodyguards, who could protect her at the cost of their own lives, had become imperative.

After the recent encounter, she could not completely trust her courtiers and the army. Didda felt insecure even inside the palace. She suspected and scrutinized everyone around her. Who were the people she could trust? And, why would they risk their lives for her? For days, Didda kept deliberating on this until one day she found a solution. Didda herself visited everyone who had saved her at the Padmaswamin temple and rewarded them with enormous offerings in return for their service.

In just a few years of her reign in Kashmir, Didda was successful in winning the hearts of people because of her good deeds that resulted in the commoner's upliftment. She herself rewarded people, and when the subjects witnessed this, the respect for their queen grew manifold. The youngsters were motivated and aspired to be a part of Didda's army. They saw her immense rewards in wealth and gold as a means to secure their future generations—it was something that no other kingdom had ever done. Every young adult aspired to receive laurels, recognitions and rewards. This did not remain hidden from the eyes of the queen. She knew these youngsters were impressionable and selective grooming could make them loyal to the crown, at least for now.

She selected them from across the kingdom, trained them and made them strong and dependable yodhas, or warriors, of her army. Didda shared her thoughts with Narvahan that she wanted to build a military training school for the youngsters.

She instructed Narvahan to groom such soldiers. However, the only condition was that they had to join of their own free will. Narvahan could not coerce them into joining the school.

Forcing someone did not make the job better, especially when someone intended to gain the trust of the other person. Didda enforced three conditions on Narvahan for the induction of the youngsters. First, that all youngsters must be poor; second, they should know every nook and corner of the place they lived; lastly, they must have at least one unique quality, such as climbing trees, swimming, climbing a mountain or imitating a bird's sound. For Narvahan, it was a huge challenge to find such young men with all the qualities laid down by Didda.

To raise such an elite army and train them, Didda thought of none other than VikramSen, her mentor and the commander-in-chief of Loharin kingdom. VikramSen's training had turned a crippled girl into a mighty queen and an exponent in all forms of warfare.

Narvahan came up with an idea. He suggested Didda that it would be better if she could have a duel match with VikramSen in front of thousands of probable young recruits who could see their queen in action. It would further motivate them to join the army. Didda found this idea worthy. She also thought that it would be a good idea to have a duel with her mentor to induce patriotism among the probables.

At the invitation of the Queen of Kashmir, VikramSen presented himself before Didda. The queen was overjoyed to see her mentor agree to combat after so many years. She welcomed him and explained to him her plan for constituting the strongest army ever for Kashmir—a special combat unit to crush rebellions. She asked him to train the new recruits and groom them into world-beaters. Narvahan also reiterated about the duel between him and the queen that would inspire and motivate the young crop to join the army. VikramSen smiled at Narvahana and said, 'How can I fight the mighty queen who has already brought the world at her feet?' Didda replied, 'I would always remain your disciple irrespective of what happens.'

On the day of the event, the stadium was filled with one thousand youngsters who had come to witness the conflict between the queen and her guru. After years, VikramSen was in front of Didda again—to see if she still remembered what he had taught her.

The guru and her student participated in various competitions from fencing to archery. Didda performed her best, fought hard against VikramSen and emerged as the winner in each of the contests.

'Didda, Didda, Didda'—the name echoed in the stadium. VikramSen was proud to see his student being one-step ahead of him in every task. The youngsters watched with awe as their queen, a disabled woman, fought so well, which, in turn, made them join the army and train under her guru. All those young men were amazed by what they had witnessed. They thought that if a crippled woman could do that, they could too. Everyone grew more and more passionate to become a warrior like Didda. Their queen had managed to achieve what she intended to by organizing this event.

At the end of the event, Narvahan had accomplished his task of successfully presenting the young recruits Didda wanted. She had the best of young warriors to choose from for her elite army.

Didda placed the young recruits under VikramSen's tutelage

for a stipulated period. She offered awards to the new recruits who completed the gruelling training and were triumphant.

The next day, before the sun rose over Kashmir, the young recruits were jolted out of their slumber for their new combat training. When they reached the ground, they found VikramSen waiting for them. He welcomed them, asked them to leave their comforts behind and get their mind and body ready for combat.

The following days would be tough and challenging, as it would test their mental and physical strength. He then explained the rules every soldier had to abide by. He said, 'Every soldier had to master four subjects in weaponry. First is Yantra-Mukta in which weapons such as bow and arrow are used. Second is Paani-Mukta—weapons which have to be thrown by hand at the enemy.' He picked up a spear and showed what a Pani-Mukta weapon looked like. 'Third is Mukta-Mukta, a weapon which can be held and also be thrown at the enemy to kill.' He picked up a Trishul and showed it to them as an example. 'Finally, the Hasta-Shastra, those weapons that are hand-held like a sword or a gada (mace).'

The next day, when the young soldiers came to the training ground, they were shown special weapons designed by VikramSen. They had to master the use of these weapons. VikramSen was very categorical and explained that without mastering these weapons, none of the recruits would be promoted to the next level of the training. He showed them the weapons one after the other.

The first one was Shakti—it had a lion's face with a sharp tongue and claws. Then, a snake-faced javelin called Tomar that had wings and could fly deep into an enemy formation. The other deadly weapons were the Paash that had winding iron wires, the Hrishti sword, a Gada that weighed 1,000 kg, a hammer called Muddar and a discus with talons called Chakra that could be thrown from a distance to wedge the enemies' necks. The young soldiers realized that they had been introduced to the weapons used in the epic war of Mahabharata, believed to be extinct until now.

VikramSen continued to surprise the soldiers with Vajra Kulish and then came the iconic and most revered Trishul— the prized weapon of Lord Shiva. Trident paved way for the pointed shool that could result in a painful death by rupturing the enemy's body when thrown from a distance. VikramSen further shocked them by drawing the fearsome sword Asi. It was widely believed to have been used by the mighty Durga herself. Then came the Khadag, the sacrificial sword that reminded everyone of Lord Yama. He also spoke about Chandrahas that Ravan, the king of Lanka, wielded. The spectacle continued with the dual-faced axe Farsa used by Parshuram and the Musaal, popular as the smaller version of the gada. Eventually, VikramSen pulled out his favourite Vaishnav weapon called Dhanush—Lord Rama's favourite. He continued to show them other weapons such as Parigh, Bandipal, Parshihu, Shanku Barchi and the Pattish, a sword with multiple iron strips.

'The ultimate weapon, however, is the Bahu-Yudha. Unless you master that, you will never be a true warrior,' VikramSen spoke with a resolute calmness that made the young soldiers all the more nervous.

No one had the courage to question VikramSen. Their young minds were anxious to know about the Bahu-Yudha. The whispers started growing louder when their trainer silenced them.

'Bahu-Yudha is the art of fighting without any weapon. It teaches you to use your body parts as tools and your mind as the master weapon,' continued VikramSen.

He, then, went on to explain the Sushrut Samhita. He said, 'It details the importance of 107 points in the human body, out of which 49 joints are considered very sensitive. An attack on any of these joints can lead to death. Our method of weapon training includes the teaching of these critical points, so you could defend your own. This is called Bahu-Yudha, or in simpler words, martial arts.'

VikramSen was a tough taskmaster. In the coming days, he did not spare anyone during the training. He ensured that everyone worked hard on skills such as leadership, military support, warfare, battle-array formation, endurance to hunger, endurance to cold, stamina and morale boosting.

The soldiers quickly realized that this was not as easy as it had seemed. It became difficult for them to sustain in front of a strict trainer such as VikramSen. Didda already knew this. She had faced these adversities during her training; she knew very well when one could break down. When the students wanted to give up, she would announce a scholarship to take care of their families. The soldiers stayed for the sake of money.

There were times when someone would ask him, 'We are only a thousand people. How can we be a force to reckon with for our enemy?'

VikramSen would explain this with instances of wars in the past. How the Spartan Lord Leonidas with only 300 men had fought against the king of Persia and managed to keep his army at bay for three days. 'The reason he could manage that was simple—he believed in himself and his potential.

The Temple Siege and the Rise of the Ekangi's 103

Leadership and self-belief are the two traits that every warrior should inculcate and nurture,' he always said.

VikramSen's way of relating swords to meditation was also interesting. He deliberated that one should love their sword so dearly that it becomes a part of them; while using a sword, one must become like a sword; when one turns quiet, one's sword should continue to do the talking. There were many such examples and anecdotes he shared during the training.

VikramSen also trained them mentally. He told his students that a true warrior must be calm within.

'A true warrior is not someone who never gets angry, but someone who knows where to use the aggression.' VikramSen was an ardent follower of Lord Krishna and would often quote him to explain the virtues a warrior must possess.

'बलं वीर्यं च तेचश्च शीघ्रता लघुहस्तता।
अविषादश्च धैर्य च पार्थान्नान्यत्र विद्यतेय़।।

The most important part was the guerrilla training. It included learning to be vicious, lying without fear, retrieving information from the enemy, confusing the enemy, isolating him and bringing him to the battlefield among other guiles.

VikramSen was training everyone in all these areas successfully.

Soon, the training was over and VajraBahu was appointed as the commander of this elite force. VikramSen sent for VajraBahu and briefed him about a Turkish warlord who had sneaked into Kashmir and his plans to attack Srinagaram. The information was that the Turks had camped in the nearby Varahmul forest. Instructions were clear and VajraBahu knew he had to prove his worth. Within hours, VajraBahu briefed the elite group about the mission and they set out to Varahmul. The soldiers swelled with pride as they set off to fight the enemies of Kashmir—their sole purpose to enroll into the army. VajraBahu and his men galloped through the dead of the night. They wanted to complete their mission before dawn because the sunrise would expose them to the Turks occupying the vantage points.

Their strategy was to move inside the forest, and then split into two teams and use the deodar trees for cover for the ground forces.

The soldiers rode along the banks of Vitasta and moved towards the forest. The decisive moment arrived when they entered the dense forest. All they had learnt about combat and everything else that these soldiers stood for was about to be put to test. Soon enough, the pathfinder found a few camps and a bonfire that had been extinguished with cinder remains.

'The Turks, perhaps, have gone off to sleep. Should we surround and attack?' a soldier whispered to VajraBahu.

'Turks sleeping in the night? And, that too in a foreign land? I hope for their own good that they are not,' VajraBahu whispered.

'Just five camps? How could it be possible?' VajraBahu kept thinking, as his eyes waged a war with his mind and VikramSen's training. It all seemed too easy so far and contradicted what he knew about these marauders.

Something went past his ear, an unusually familiar sound. VajraBahu's face transfixed with horror as the soldier next to him fell with an arrow pierced through his neck. The soldier could not even scream. VajraBahu's worst fears came true and he swiftly ordered all to take cover. Just above them, a volley of arrows began to shower in through the dark skies—it was an ambush.

The Temple Siege and the Rise of the Ekangi's

VajraBahu's soldiers were put to test—their values and their valour challenged by forces hidden in the dark. One after the other, they fell to the arrows. VajraBahu signalled for them to retreat and reorganize. He signalled for counter formation and they began shooting upwards at the trees. VajraBahu noticed the arrows were piercing from a vertical angle—the enemy had to be up in the trees. His own soldiers who had sneaked up in the trees gradually got accustomed to the darkness and started the counteroffensive. VajraBahu realized that they were surrounded. The only way out was to abandon and retreat. That, however, was not an option for him, but some soldiers did begin to retreat. VajraBahu ordered for everyone to fall back and fight until death. Some did not need him to say so, but some began to run away, taking the same route they did to reach the Turk camps. Screams and fear filled the dense forest.

Amidst the wails, something strange happened. The incessant volley of arrows stopped raining on VajraBahu and his men stood their ground. A familiar drumroll began to echo. It was a message! VajraBahu heaped a sigh of relief. This drumroll was a sign of approaching friendly troops. The drumroll was a signal to stop the assault.

The arrows had stopped, and faces began to emerge from the darkness. One particular face sent shivers down VajraBahu's spine. It was VikramSen.

Soon, they were face to face and VajraBahu's mind turned blank. Why would VikramSen entrap his own soldiers—the elite group that he himself had created and trained? Why this brutal killing?

VikramSen read his emotions, raised his sword and signalled. VajraBahu felt the ground beneath him tremble as the volley of arrows began again. This time, they were targetted at the soldiers who were retreating. VajraBahu stood in shock as he realized this was culling, the ancient tradition of identifying the sheep among men. Soldiers who could not uphold the values were being killed. VikramSen was baptizing his soldiers. The final training was over. The glorious few who survived were the men who would be wearing the crescent moon. These men would not hesitate to sacrifice their lives to save their kingdom.

Didda was extremely happy with their performance. The kingdom of Kashmir had witnessed their bravery and exceptional spirit. The entire nation was proud of these 500 soldiers.

Didda and VikramSen felicitated these elite soldiers. VikramSen also announced in the royal court that the army of these soldiers would be given a special title and a flag.

'They have been trained to align their body, soul and weapon as one. It will be apt to call them Ekangior, rather than Didda's Ekangi Sena.'

The royal court accepted the title and applauded. They would never be separated from Didda. She then launched a massive undercover campaign to identify and crush rebel. Soon, Narvahan secured a victory over the rest. She ruthlessly killed many of the rebels, including her husband's nephews, but forgave those who repented and sought mercy. On the other hand, Didda kept up the pressure on Abhimanyu and his trainers, so that he could learn the art of combat. When she was informed that Abhimanyu was ready, she ensured that she was present for his final test—a sword test.

Abhimanyu was in awe for her presence during the test, but Didda got furious and lamented that as a king on the

The Temple Siege and the Rise of the Ekangi's 107

battlefield, he can't afford to be sentimental. She was enraged at the trainers for the dismal performance of the prince.

She realized that she needed someone else. She summoned VikramSen once again and told him of the special task that she wanted him to complete. She wanted him to train the future king of Kashmir. Didda supervised his training herself. Very soon, she was told that Abhimanyu was now ready to be the king. It was time for Didda to test the future king herself. As was her way, the true way of a warrior, Didda summoned Abhimanyu to fight her.

Abhimanyu fought gallantly with the queen to prove his mettle, and to show her that he had grown up to be a great warrior. With a sharp swipe of his blade, he had his sword at Didda's neck—he had won and proven himself. Later that evening, VikramSen sought permission to see the queen. He fell at the feet of the queen while she was clearing her wounds and sought forgiveness, much to her amazement. He told Didda that he had failed in his duty and was ashamed that the prince could not be trained, as she had desired. Didda drew her sword in a flash and placed it on VikramSen's neck—a shocked VikramSen stared at his impending death.

6

The New Prince and the Regent

VikramSen realized that the queen had purposely allowed the prince to win. He knew that Didda was far beyond the dexterity of the young Prince Abhimanyu, as he, himself, had trained Didda to be a warrior whose sword and skill had no match. He confronted the queen and asked, 'Why? Why did you surrender? Why did you belittle my teaching? You are one of the finest warriors I have ever seen, and I have always been proud that I was your teacher. Then, why did you surrender? Did your motherly feelings win over the great Queen Didda's decision-making capabilities? Did you lose on purpose?'

Didda was silent. VikramSen thundered in angst, 'Why Didda?' Didda looked at VikramSen with smoldering eyes, 'Swear on me, you will not utter a word about this to another living person or I will have you beheaded forgetting that you are my mentor.' VikramSen stood helpless, seething with displeasure at his beloved pupil who was hell-bent on destroying her glory.

Didda looked at him and understood the inner turmoil his mentor was going through. She stared out of the window, into infinity and beyond, and then taking a deep breath, sighed

The New Prince and the Regent 109

and said softly, 'Kashmir needs a king.' She took a pause and whispered, 'Not a queen. Had Abhimanyu failed today, he would never have become the king. He would have fallen from grace and the people of Kashmir would never have accepted a disgraced man as their king.'

She held VikramSen's hands in hers and said, 'The reason I called you to train Abhimanyu was to create an aura, the confidence in him and in the people of this kingdom, that he was being trained to become a deadly warrior and a great king. Under your tutelage, he has grown to be a good prince, and hopefully one day, he will become a great king.'

VikramSen tried to intervene, 'But...'

Before he could finish his sentence, Didda added, 'Also, it would serve the male ego of the powerful warlords and noblemen as they would be honoured to serve a king than a queen, or, in my case, a crippled queen.' Didda said with a smirk on her face.

VikramSen was at a loss; he had no answer for his beloved queen. All his anger and displeasure gave way to tears as he saw the end of an era in front of him. The queen who had single-handedly revived the fortunes of a failing kingdom was today falling prey to the age-old traditions of not accepting a crippled queen as a ruler.

As the sun arose over Kashmir, a new dawn was about to set in. Didda sent summons to all the courtiers and chieftains for a special court meeting. There was a buzz in the kingdom as the word spread that Didda was going to make a special announcement, but nobody knew what it would be. The courtroom was brimming with people as Didda strolled in with Valaga by her side. She took her seat and looked at the people as they shouted, 'Long live Queen Didda'. The crowd became quiet as she stood up to speak, 'Today is a very significant day for me and for our kingdom. Today, Kashmir will have a new king. As you all know, Prince AbhimanyuGupt has come of age. So, without further ado, I anoint the official heir to the throne—AbhimanyuGupt as the king of Kashmir.'

There was absolute silence inside the court. There was no eruption of cheers to celebrate the nomination of the new king, as one would have expected. Queen Didda had won so much respect and love from the people that they could not accept anyone else as their ruler.

After what felt like ages, one of the courtiers stood up and broke the silence, 'Long live King AbhimanyuGupt! Long live Kashmir! Long live Queen Didda!' Slowly, one by one, the courtroom picked the slogan and the whole court now echoed with this acclamation for the new king. Queen Didda raised her hand and the people fell silent once again.

She looked at Narvahan and said, 'I ask Prime Minister Narvahan to find an appropriate date for the coronation of our new king and let the whole kingdom celebrate. Decorate the city like a bride. Send invitations to all the kingdoms and the noblemen to witness this momentous event of Kashmir.'

Didda beckoned Abhimanyu who has been sitting among the courtiers to come to her. Abhimanyu went to the queen and touched her feet for blessings. Didda held him by the shoulders and said, 'No, now you are the king. You should not bow down in front of anybody.'

Abhimnayu said, 'But, you are my mother.'

Didda replied, 'I am your mother in the palace. Here, in court, you are the king and I am your subject. Always remember that.'

She made Abhimanyu stand by her side, raised his hand and shouted, 'Hail the new King AbhimanyuGupt.'

The whole court reverberated with the slogan, 'Hail the new King AbhimanyuGupt.'

As everybody cheered for the new king, one man stood silently in a corner, witnessing the whole scene and drowning in profound melancholy... It was VikramSen.

As the queen settled down in her chamber after the hectic activity in the court, Valaga informed her that a messenger from Kabul, representing her grandfather King Bheem, was waiting for her.

'Usher him in quickly,' said Didda.

The messenger bowed in front of Didda.

'Tell me what message you bring from my motherland,' asked Didda, dreading that it was not something ominous.

'My queen, I have bad news to report,' replied the messenger.

'Speak up quickly,' thundered Didda, losing her composure, which was very unlikely of her—the queen who had always maintained a stoic composure, even in the direst of situations.

'My queen... King Bheem's health is deteriorating. The royal physicians are not very hopeful. They have requested you to visit him as the king is in his last stages,' the messenger said softly.

Hearing the news, Didda was taken aback. On this auspicious day, when she had just anointed her son as the next king, she didn't expect to hear the news of her grandfather being on his deathbed. In fact, that was the last thing she expected to hear.

Once again, she found herself at crossroads—whether she must celebrate her son's appointment as the new king or visit her ailing grandfather who loved her more than her father. Life had always put her on such thresholds where she had to make difficult choices. When the messenger left, she asked Valaga to call Narvahan, her trusted lieutenant and friend who had always advised her wisely in all dire circumstances.

Narvahan hurried up to her chamber. Valaga announced the arrival of Narvahan, 'My queen, Minister Narvahan is here.'

As Narvahan was ushered into the chamber, he saw the queen's low-spirited face in the light of the lamps. Narvahan was apprehensive to see the queen in this state.

'My queen, what troubles you so much to make you look so desolate?' asked a nervous Narvahan.

Didda looked at him and gave a bleak smile, 'Why do I have to always make choices? Why does life always put me on crossroads?'

'Because you are the bravest and the noblest... and because as a queen, through your acts you inspire people to fight their adversities and emerge victorious,' replied Narvahan.

'But, at the end of the day, I am also a human being made of blood and flesh. How long do you think I can continue like this?' asked Didda.

Realizing that her queen was going through an inner turmoil, the minister asked, 'What is the cause of such distress, my queen?'

'A messenger from Kabul just brought in the news of my ailing grandfather, King Bheem. He is breathing his last and wishes to see me,' answered Didda.

'That's indeed very disheartening to hear, my queen,' replied Narvahan.

'On one hand, it is the coronation of my son who is set to become king. If I leave for Kabul, I won't be able to witness the most beautiful event of my son's life—becoming the king of Kashmir. But, if I stay back, I would probably live with this guilt of not seeing my grandfather when he was on his deathbed and was beckoning me to go and meet him. I am facing a moral dilemma between my duty and the love for my son. Hence, I called for you, so you can wisely advise me in this adverse situation.'

After a long pause, Narvahan said, 'I understand your dilemma, my queen. In this situation, I would advise you to decide as a queen and not as a mother or a granddaughter. Under the current circumstances and as a queen, your first responsibility is towards your kingdom which calls on you to appoint the heir to the throne. If you don't attend the coronation ceremony, it would send a wrong signal to the warlords who are waiting for any opportunity to harm the kingdom. It would convey that the king doesn't have your blessing, and the fear that you have created in their hearts would be gone in an instant. Your departure will also demoralize the army. They are strong but without your sound leadership, they may become vulnerable to the enemy's advantage. In the event of a war, King Abhimanyu will face a dearth of battle experience. So, my advice would be to attend the coronation, usher in the new regime and then proceed to Kabul.'

'You speak wisely, Narvahan,' replied Didda.

Once alone in her chamber, Didda was still in a solemn mood contemplating the day's events. She thought about her son becoming the king, the promise that she had made to her dying husband KshemGupt of providing an able king to Kashmir and about her grandfather who always loved her, no matter how the world treated her. On one hand was the significant event that would secure the future of her kingdom, and on the other hand was the past—both coaxing her to decide. Narvahan's advice made complete sense, but she was still being pulled by her grandfather's love to go see him. When Valaga came in with food, she refused to have even a morsel.

Valaga understood the dilemma Didda was in. When Didda refused to have food again, Valaga said, 'If it hurts you so much, then go and visit your grandfather first. He is the one who has loved you selflessly. At least you owe him this much in his last days. As far as your son is concerned, you have already announced that he is the new king; it is as good as the coronation; now, only the formalities remain. And even if you don't attend the formalities, he would be still coronated as the king. But, if your grandfather dies, he will not come back which would haunt you for days to come.'

'You are right in your feelings, Valaga, but being the queen, I cannot take decisions based on emotions. Leave me alone for some time whilst I come to some conclusion,' said Didda and retreated to the inner chamber leaving Valaga.

As she paced in her chamber mulling over the events of the day, she could not come up with any decision. The only person, she thought, who could bring her out of this dilemma was her guru, AbhinavGupt. She decided to pay him a visit and at that very moment, all the ambiguity clouding her mind cleared up. She called for Valaga and asked to be taken to him immediately.

As she reached AbhinavGupt's abode, she found him immersed in meditation. She asked her maids and guards to leave her and Valaga while they waited for her guru to complete his meditation.

The New Prince and the Regent 115

After some time, as AbhinavGupt opened his eyes, he found Queen Didda and Valaga sitting in front of him. As soon as Didda saw that AbhinavGupta had opened his eyes, she offered him oblations by placing flowers in front of him. AbhinavGupt got up from his seat and held Didda by her shoulders, asking her to get up.

'My queen, what brings you here at this hour?' asked AbhinavGupt.

'Guruji...' and with a quiver in her voice, Didda explained the dilemma of being caught in-between her duties of a queen, a mother and a granddaughter.

'Narvahan has advised me to follow the raj dharma, Valaga tells me to follow my heart. But I don't know...' submitted Didda.

'My queen, Narvahan is indeed a wise man. Complete the coronation ceremony and then leave for Kabul immediately. I will also accompany you,' replied AbhinavGupt.

'Thank you for clearing my doubts, but I am unable to understand the reason for you to come to Kabul with me,' asked Didda.

AbhinavGupt gave a smile and said, 'Let the time come and I will tell you. Now go and get some rest, as tomorrow you have a hectic day ahead of you.'

Didda and Valaga took leave from AbhinavGupt. As he watched them depart, he smiled to himself, 'Didda, your journey is not yet over, you have a long way to go. Destiny awaits you.'

As the sun rose over the mountains, a new chapter was about to unfold in the history of Kashmir. A new king was going to get anointed after a long time. The whole of Kashmir was in the mood of jubilation and festivity. Kings and noblemen from far and nearby lands were invited to attend this majestic event—the coronation of King AbhimanyuGupt. Didda had left no stone unturned in making this a stupendous event replete with fervour and festivity. She had made sure that all the kings of nearby kingdoms came and paid obeisance to the new king. Be it out of fear or out of respect for Didda, all the kings did make their way for the coronation. Pundits from various parts of India were called. The water from all the holy rivers of India were brought in golden vessels. The kingdom was decorated like a newly-wed bride.

On the *muhurta,* or auspicious time, Prince Abhimanyu was anointed as the new king of Kashmir. Didda herself placed the crown on the new king's head after which she stood proudly on the podium of the majestic palace of Kashmir and exclaimed to the awaiting subjects, 'Long live King AbhimanyuGupt!'

The whole palace suddenly started to reverberate with the sounds of celebration for the new king, 'Long live King AbhimanyuGupt!'

As the festivities of the newly-crowned king was going on, AbhinavGupt advised Didda to proceed for Kabul on the first day of the poornima so she could be there at the doorsteps of Kabul on amavas.

'What about the dark night?' Didda was curious to know but AbhinavGupt only smiled in return. His smile put Didda in a pensive mood and she wondered about the darkness that lay ahead.

Didda set out on an arduous fortnight-long journey to Kabul along with her trusted shadow, Valaga, her Ekangi army and her guru, AbhinavGupt.

The New Prince and the Regent 117

Inside the palace of Kabul, King BheemShah was supine on his bed. Perhaps it was the first time ever that he had laid down for so many days. He had never rested in his life, until now. His granddaughter Didda, sat beside him, worried about his health. AbhinavGupt, the most renowned spiritual master of the century was engrossed in the calculation of planets, stars and time. Didda keenly observed him as he drew several crisscrossing lines on a platter of vermillion. After concluding his exhaustive calculations, AbhinavGupt solemnly asked BheemShah what his last wish would be.

Didda's vision blurred as her eyes brimmed with tears at AbhinavGupt's question. BheemShah was the only one who loved Didda unconditionally, even more than Valaga did. All her hardships used to get resolved under his benevolent shield. But, this one question seemed to rob her of everything.

Lying down in his bed, BheemShah expressed his gratitude to AbhinavGupt with folded hands. The news of his imminent death brought no distress to him. He had lived well. On seeing Didda's sad face, he pulled her close to him and asked, 'Would you remain sad like this or arrange for your grandfather's last wish?'

With a feeble smile, Didda respectfully asked him about his last wish. He said, 'I want all the aghoris in the Shiva temples of Kabul to perform a Maharudrabhishek. Lord Shiva dwells in the blessings of the aghoris. I want to invoke their blessings so that I don't have to worry about the protection of our kingdom anymore.'

Didda was deeply touched by her grandfather's concern for the land's security even when he lay on his deathbed. She immediately extended her hand to promise her grandfather but was interrupted by AbhinavGupt, 'You do not have that much time.'

'How much time does he have?' asked a worried Didda.

'Three hours,' replied AbhinavGupt solemnly.

Didda's eyes were moist and she struggled to hold back her tears by looking up. She sat there holding her grandfather's hand. Upon hearing AbhinavGupt's proclamation, BheemShah miraculously experienced a flow of energy. He stepped down from his bed and said, 'Lord Shiva is being kind to me. He is calling me soon. Arrange for Lord Shiva's invocation in the palace. I wish to leave for the heavenly abode chanting his name. Arrange for my anointment!'

The entire palace took to attending to his wishes. Didda supervised all the chores while the entire royal family began assembling around the king. Eleven Brahmins began preparations for the sacred pooja. All the nooks and corners of the palace reverberated with the chants of '*Om namah Shivay*'. Oil and turmeric paste were applied to the king. Then, he was bathed in water that was infused with herbs. Sandalwood paste was applied on his forehead, followed by various perfumes. Finally, he was draped in the finest attires made out of rare Kashmir mulberry silk. Though everyone was grieving in their hearts, they took care of his smallest wishes.

At the altar of the Shiva temple within the palace, a fire was lit with sandalwood and camphor. BheemShah took his seat in front of Lord Shiva. He looked into the Lord's kind eyes and sang the Shivstuti with great devotion.

As BheemShah continued to sing the hymn, a strange energy filled his body. The Shiva idol in front of him appeared to come to life. BheemShah witnessed Lord Shiva performing the cosmic dance as Nataraja amidst the flames. He felt drawn to the flames as if the Lord himself had come to take him away. As the hymns began reaching a crescendo, an enchanted BheemShah began moving towards the Lord. Didda appeared to have sensed the intention of King BheemShah and she rushed to stop him, but AbhinavGupt immediately came forward and held her back. Didda was shocked and looked at her guru with pleading eyes. But AbhinavGupt did not relent. Bowing to her guru's command, a helpless Didda stopped. She now hoped and prayed to the Lord. She looked desolately at her grandfather who was walking towards his death. The entire palace was perplexed by this. Oblivious to the anxiety all around him, BheemShah kept moving towards the fire, chanting the hymn of Shiva all along. As he found himself closer to Shiva's image, he became oblivious of the world around him. Tears of joy started to flow down his face. The scorching flames no longer scared him. Didda tried one more time to move but found herself helpless in the clutches of her guru. All she could do was squawk as she saw BheemShah put his foot in the enormous havan kund. His delicate mulberry silk melted away and his body was engulfed in the fire, but BheemShah's face was bereft of emotions. It appeared as if he had been waiting for this moment for long. His soul was desperate to merge with Shiva's leaving the body behind. He was now inside the havan kund. The leaping flames engulfed him and gradually the mass of flesh and bones burnt to ashes, as was the way of Shiva. Didda could hold herself back no longer and felt dizzy. The agony of losing another person who had truly loved her was unbearable.

People of Kabul bowed their heads with great reverence

120 Didda: The Warrior Queen of Kashmir

as a mark of solemn respect on King BheemShah's demise.

News of BheemShah's death spread like wildfire within and outside Hindustan. Kings and emperors from the mainland immediately reached Kabul to express their condolences. However, this news brought a wave of cheer to the Ziyarid dynasty outside the borders of Hindustan. The once extensive kingdom of Iran was now fragmented into small estates and regimes.

The Ziyarid dynasty ruled over Tabaristan. On hearing about the demise of Hindushahi King BheemShah, Ziyarid King Wushmagir saw the opportunity that he had been waiting for a long time. To conquer Kabul had been his dream. No one could dare even look at Kabul under BheemShah's rule, but now, the situation was different.

There was no one who could challenge the might of Wushamgir. Along with his Commander-in-Chief Abu Mohammad, Wushmagir drew a strategy to attack Kabul. He felt BheemShah's successor, Prince Jaipal, was no match for him. His commander would be enough for the prince. With this thought, Wushmagir sent his huge army, under the command of Abu Mohammed, marching towards Kabul to conquer it. The stage was set for an epic battle across the great central Asian plains. Yet another piece of history was waiting to be etched, and then forgotten, in the near future.

Didda was busy in the rituals of her grandfather's Dashkriya, or funeral. Men and women with their families had come from near and far to offer their condolences to the deceased ruler of Kabul. In the midst of this, a spy from Didda's Ekangi army brought the news of Abu Mohammad marching towards Kabul with his large army. Didda was grieving over her grandfather's

The New Prince and the Regent 121

demise, but destiny was not going to give her the luxury of time. This news was also an opportunity for Didda to come out of the grief and funnel her deep-rooted anger.

Even though Kabul was capable of quelling any attack, but today was a precarious day. Bereft of their commander-in-chief, Kabul was vulnerable. Neither SimhRaj, nor the newly-crowned King Jaipal was capable of fending the macabre onslaught of Abu Mohammad. Didda knew that Persian control of Kabul could cast dark shadows of war on Kashmir as the two kingdoms shared their borders.

Time was of the essence, and Didda was facing an unusual situation. She, once again, sought the wise counsel of her guru AbhinavGupt. She was grateful that providence had rewarded her with a guru whose guidance always took her to greater heights. That night too something similar happened.

When Didda went to meet her guru AbhinavGupt, he did not have to be told what worried her. He gave her one more life-changing mantra that night. He said, 'Morale of the Shahi army is low, the very mention of the Persian attack will crumble them. There is no capable leadership after King BheemShah. The populace is also bewildered with these abrupt turn of events. In such a situation, everyone looks for someone on whom they could place their trust. You have that capability. I know that; but to make the world accept it, you will have to do something extraordinary.'

'Extraordinary? This is a calamity, Your Eminence,' exclaimed Didda.

'Just imagine what will happen if you save Kabul from this onslaught. If you are able to turn this calamity into an opportunity, the world will accept your supremacy. You will get the unencumbered status of the Saamraagyi,' spoke the resolute sorcerer. This gurumantra gave a new direction to Didda's thoughts.

Didda was a protégé of her grandfather's tutelage. So, intelligence, quick decision-making capability and precise execution of a combat strategy were engrained in her. Didda did not let any of her family members know about the impending Persian threat on Kabul. As soon as the rituals concluded, she, along with her Ekangi army, immediately marched towards Bamiyan in the dead of the night. AbhinavGupt was also a part of this cavalcade. Many in the family did not approve of her leaving so abruptly, but she had stopped paying heed to the world a long time ago. In addition, she knew that waiting until the thirteenth day of her grandfather's funeral ceremony would have jeopardized her plan to defend Kabul. However, King SimhRaj knew that Queen Didda's actions were never illogical or whimsical.

Overnight, they covered the distance to Bamiyan as advised by AbhinavGupt. Defeating Abu Mohammad would be an apt and true homage to her grandfather.

On the other side of Kabul, Abu Mohammad had left from Iran. Not many knew that he didn't want to conquer Kabul, but his eyes were set on Hindustan. Kabul was just the first step, and then Kashmir would act as the gateway to his siege on Hindustan. Abu was aware of the glory that awaited him on the other side of Kabul. His army was already high on the thoughts of conquering the golden goose called Hindustan. They had regularly heard about its prosperity. Invading Hindustan was their ultimate goal for which they had waited for nearly 300 years.

Abu Mohammad promised his King Wushmagir, 'You are sending me to win over Kabul. I will not only capture BheemShah's Kabul, but along with it, I would also gift you his daughter's kingdom of Loharin.'

'I have also heard that BheemShah's granddaughter is extraordinarily beautiful?' Wushmagir asked lecherously.

'What would you do with a crippled horse?' laughed Abu.

'But, if you so desire, I could present the kingdom of Kashmir at your service, which is much more beautiful than she is.' Together they ridiculed the queen's disability.

As he bade goodbye to his army, King Wushmagir filled his army with verve and vigour of annihilating Hindustan completely, and with the promise that they would soon dine together in the beautiful valley of Kashmir. All of them marched off with a newfound zeal. In comparison to these brutal, ferocious and savage warriors, Didda's army appeared to be far less in number and far too meek.

In Bamiyan, Didda was engrossed in discussion with AbhinavGupt and Narvahan. Narvhana was concerned because of the waning morale of the army in BheemShah's absence. But Didda's face did not reflect any trace of such worries. She was not worried about the war; she was engrossed in planning to win. However, Narvahan was deeply worried because this did not seem like a war but appeared to be a suicide mission.

Didda pored over the war map and the areas around Bamiyan. Something unusual was going on in her mind. She planned to hold the enemy in Bamiyan. Her chain of thoughts was interrupted when a messenger came in, 'My queen, it is not just Kabul, we just came to know that Lohar, and Kashmir too, will be invaded soon... And then, the whole of Hindustan.' The messenger wanted to say more but his hesitation was apparent.

This was the news that Didda dreaded to hear.

AbhinavGupt intervened and looked straight into her eyes, 'This messenger would not be able to describe the insults cast upon his queen's disability.' AbhinavGupt told Didda. Didda's eyes spew out lava as she said, 'Not even a bird can fly over Kashmir without my permission. How dare these invaders lay sight on my Kashmir! I might have given them Bamiyan but not an inch anymore.'

She ordered Narvahan, 'Alert the army to further strengthen the security. They must regularly inspect and reinforce the security arrangements.'

Pointing at the map of Kabul and Bamiyan, Narvahan questioned, 'We should be here, on Kabul's borders. What are we doing across the border in Bamiyan?

Didda announced, 'A ceremonial ritual has to be carried out here in Bamiyan. Assemble all the aghoris here that you can find across Kabul and Kashmir.'

She personally went around Bamiyan with AbhinavGupt and Narvahan, directing the plan of action for the ritual to ensure that nothing was left to chance. Narvahan was confused, but his faith on the wisdom of Didda was all that he had.

In two days, Bamiyan was spilling over with aghoris from all over northern India. There was no space left to set foot. Didda personally inspected the preparations for the rituals as practised by her grandfather as well as the readiness of the army.

She also inspected the security of the palace. Meanwhile, she reiterated to the newly-crowned King Jaipal that the late King BheemShah had chosen him as his successor because of

The New Prince and the Regent 125

his capabilities. He would have to show his proficiency and strength whenever the situation would arise. She was indirectly preparing Jaipal for the upcoming battle.

On the third day in Bamiyan, AbhinavGupt convened all the aghoris and started an elaborate and massive tantric ceremony. It was a sight to behold—an ensemble of aghoris and the greatest sorcerer ever to lead them. Lord Shiva himself seemed to have descended to accept the gratitude of his ardent worshipers.

AbhinavGupt had begun chanting the hymns in his deep baritone voice and nothing but Mahakaal in his fiery eyes. Trident-bearing aghoris began performing the *tandav* (the divine dance by Shiva) in front of the idol of Lord Shiva.

While Bamiyan was invigorated and invoked with the sound of the rituals performed by the AbhinavGupt, King Wushmagir's army led by Abu quietly reached Bamiyan. They entered the city and went past the aghoris who were immersed in their oblation to Shiva. Abu's men laughed at the aghoris, their rituals and frenzied dancing. The aghoris were too immersed in their devotion to notice the arrival of an army. Instead, they gave the army a safe passage. Soon, King Wushamgir's army crossed over and camped on the outskirts of Bamiyan. Kabul was just a few miles away. Just one night that separated them from their coveted prize, the crown of Kabul. They were prepared to attack Kabul the next day.

In the dark of the night, Abu rejoiced his impending victory the next day. Just then, his messenger informed him that Queen Didda's envoy had come with her message. He conveyed that the queen was desirous of a rendezvous. Abu already felt victorious, he thought half the battle had been won. He taunted the Kabul regency, 'Has BheemShah's death left Kabul devoid of men? Why is a woman being sent for a peace pact?'

The messenger nonchalantly explained, 'According to Hindu tenets, the king's son cannot partake in any activity until the entire funeral rites have been performed.'

Abu further stultified, 'Or is it that the men of Kabul negotiate hiding behind the beauty of their women? If that is so, then tell them that even our slaves are much more beautiful than their queen. Such tactics are not going to work on us.'

The emissary displayed exemplary calm and replied, 'Queen Didda was expecting such an answer from you. That is why she has already sent a reply for you—Meet just one daughter of Kabul and there would be no need to meet their men.' Abu was infuriated with this message and retorted, 'Now, I must meet your queen!'

An enraged and humiliated Abu spent a vengeful restless night waiting for dawn to break.

In the morning, at Bamiyan, AbhinavGupt commenced the anointment of Lord Shiva according to the tantric rituals with great fervour. In synchronization with the rhythm, the queen dressed as a warrior with her fifteen warriors. With Narvahan, she galloped to keep her tryst with Abu at his camp. Tearing her way through the crowds and the clamour of aghoris, Didda reached Abu's camp. Abu's soldiers were astounded to see the speed with which she was approaching the cantonment. Didda had also sized up Abu's army as she cantered past them. Each one of them was tall and muscular. Combat and warfare seemed to be gushing in their blood and they too seemed to be watching her fiercely. Didda's eyes observed every minute detail—their cavalry, elephants' regiment and everything else.

Abu, a seven-feet-tall warrior, was impressed with Didda's valour and pace. Still astride her horse, Didda gestured Narvahan to convey her message. Narvahan addressed Abu with great impertinence, 'We have come to forewarn you that this is our land. We have no inclination for a war; but if we resolve to fight, we shall not stop till we put an end to your penchant for belligerence. It will be best if you retreat before stepping foot on the soil of Kabul. We promise you a safe exit if you decide to leave peacefully and now.'

Abu was astounded by Narvahan's speech. He had expected Didda to plead for peace. Instead, she came to challenge Abu's military might and his vainglorious ego contemptuously along with just a handful of fifteen soldiers in tow. Abu walked up to Narvahan and shouted, 'Does your queen really have so much fire or...'

Even before Abu could complete his sentence, four soldiers surrounded him with their swords ready to slash his neck. Immediately, Abu's security cordon sprang into action encircling those four. But none of Didda's men were perturbed. Disregarding Abu's men, they vaulted on their horses with a bat of an eye. Abu's soldiers were taken aback seeing the swiftness and agility of Didda's soldiers. All the fifteen soldiers yelled in unison, dauntlessly warning Abu to either pull back or face dire consequences. They did not wait for Abu's reactions, and hailing Goddess Bhawani, the soldiers galloped out from there.

Abu was enraged, 'She has the audacity to challenge me on my own turf and leave in one piece.' He ordered his forces to surround Didda. One platoon of his army circled Didda's fifteen soldiers. All their exit routes were sealed, and they were surrounded. But, Didda's men were doughty. Before

Abu's men could even realize what was happening, the whole platoon was annihilated. Didda's Ekangi's ruthlessly butchered the platoon.

Abu was unable to fathom what he had witnessed. He was still trying to come to terms with the situation that had suddenly taken such an unprecedented turn right in front of him. He had come all the way from Iran with his mighty barbaric army just to find himself besieged by a band of fifteen soldiers and a crippled woman. Suddenly, he felt his life was in jeopardy. Didda stood in front of Abu and saw the terror and pain on his face. In those intricate moments of life or death, her beauty dazzled Abu as she came close. Astride her horse, Didda said, 'We were leaving after we made an offer of peace. You betrayed us, but still, I am giving you one more chance, LEAVE!'

She spurred her horse to gallop. As she raced past Abu, she shouted, 'Run away, save yourself or else I will have your head paraded through Iran on a spike.' Didda's troop followed her as swiftly.

That moment when Didda asked him to flee played again and again on Abhu's mind. Abu found himself extremely humiliated and waited for his turn to retaliate. As soon as he found himself safe within his security ring, he shouted, 'ATTACK!'

Didda heard his war cry; she had anticipated this. As planned, her ploy about peace had made Abu's men complacent today. Secondly, a glimpse of the military prowess of just fifteen soldiers had certainly lowered the confidence of Abu's army. They were left in awe of the daring acts of this small troop.

'We have heard about the valour of BheemShah's army. Therefore, what if he himself is not there. His gritty soldiers will come charging. Our martyrdom is warranted,' Abu's soldiers whispered to each other.

Didda's third ploy was about to unravel now. Abu's messenger had informed him that Didda's army was still in Kabul. Only fifteen soldiers were accompanying her for peace negotiations. Everyone was about to be proven wrong. The moment Didda heard Abu's war cry, all her fifteen soldiers chanted loudly, '*Har Har Mahadev*'.

As the air echoed with Didda's chants, thousands of aghoris sprang out of their trance. The sky above Bamiyan was filled with the war cries of aghoris—Har Har Mahadev. Abu and his soldiers were bewildered with the cascading turn of events, one after the other. They found themselves in Didda's web as thousands of aghoris laid siege on them. What the invaders didn't realize was that these aghoris were savage fighters from Didda's Ekangi. They had entered Bamiyan in the guise of aghoris. History had just witnessed its first instance of guerrilla warfare.

A fierce battle erupted. The queen was herself commanding her forces in the battlefield.

Due to the of the martial prowess imparted by Queen Didda, her 1,000 warriors weighed heavy against the 30,000 soldiers of Abu Mohammad. His men were unable to ascertain the direction of the enemies' charges and their strategies. She was soon engaged in a one-on-one battle with Abu, proving more than a match to him. Twice, her sword blade gashed upon Abu's neck. His lieutenants also came to his rescue and fought with Didda. In this rapacious battle, Abu escaped from the battlefield. This fierce battle ensued for the next forty minutes. The brown terrain of Bamiyan soon turned into a crimson sea of blood. Thousands of corpses lay strewn all over.

'Don't spare even a single enemy. Not an inch, not a limb,'

Didda could be heard roaring like a tigress. Didda and her Ekangi's did not stop until the only pair of limbs attached to its body belonged to Abu who was holed up inside one of the demolished camps.

The triumphant queen ordered the camps to be set on fire. Escaping from the inferno, Abu found himself in front of Didda. While his face was struck with terror, Didda's glowed with victory. With supreme swiftness, Didda dismounted from her stallion. It was hard to believe that she was crippled. Wielding her sword, she lunged towards Abu. He found himself cornered and unable to comprehend the chain of events. He immediately surrendered and begged for mercy.

Stamping on his face with her crippled leg, Didda hissed, 'This lame mare cannot help you anymore.'

Narvahan reminded her, 'A surrendered enemy is always to be pardoned.'

On hearing this, a flicker of hope flashed in Abu's eyes. He looked up at Didda to seek mercy. Didda trampled on him with even greater force and reminded Narvahan, 'A condoned and wounded enemy strikes back with double the force!'

In an arresting voice, she told Abu Mohammad, 'You were pardoned twice earlier, yet you backstabbed like a coward. You will have to pay for this dastardly act now!'

Didda signalled a mahout who goaded his elephant towards the centre. Abu was thrown in front of the elephant. He tried hard to save himself but was trampled to death by the pachyderm.

Once again, atop her stallion, with a fluttering saffron flag in her hand and hailing Goddess Bhawani, the victorious Didda galloped towards the Bamiyan temple to seek her mentor's blessings.

7

Narvahan's Death and the End of an Era

The kingdom of Kashmir echoed with the sounds of 'Har Har Mahadev' as Didda returned victorious from the battle against the commander-in-chief of Iran. The kingdom celebrated her valour while the queen locked herself in her chamber.

Narvahan paid her a visit to greet her. 'Congratulations, my queen, for leading us in this emphatic victory.' Narvahan said exuberantly.

'What victory, Narvahan? War, bloodshed, deaths—is this what you call victory? Why can't there be peace?' Didda lamented with grief that she had held in her heart since long. It seemed as if she had been waiting for Narvahan to ask her this question to vent her inner turmoil with one of her most trusted friends.

'Peace? There is no peace in the life of a warrior queen. And a warrior, like you, should be proud of the feat you have achieved,' replied Narvahan.

'What should I be proud of, Narvahan? What good have I ever got in my life? First, the gods were not kind enough and made me a cripple. Since my birth, everyone has neglected me. My parents left me in the hands of Valaga. I never got the love I wanted, I deserved, from them. Being a warrior was never a choice but a condition to get some attention from my father, to prove my worth in front of him,' said Didda bitterly.

'But, see how well you have proved yourself. You've shown everyone that because of your courage and strength, you are no less than anybody.'

'But Narvahan, why do I have to prove myself every time. Is it because I am a woman? I never wanted to be a warrior. Nevertheless, I have had to fight and win every war, for if I lose, the same kingdom, which takes pride in my victories, shall criticize my womanhood because everyone believes that a woman is weak. My courtiers conspire against me, for they do not want to be ruled by a woman. My enemies see me as an easy prey. They want both my kingdom and me. And, every time I have had to fight a war to prove myself, my worth, to my kingdom, to the court and even to my family.'

She shook her head and with a sigh continued, 'They say that Shiva also needs Shakti to be complete. They worship Shakti, they worship Kali and yet, they still can't see me—a woman—rule over them.'

'I do understand your angst, my queen; but you have shown that a woman is no less. You have become a reflection of the Shakti herself. At every step, you have given everyone a reason to love you.'

'But, why can't I be loved for no reason at all? My parents did not love me. The kingdom and the Rajmata only love me because I am the mother of their heir. My parents also started loving me when I became a mother of the crown prince.

Narvahan's Death and the End of an Era   133

Everyone is selfish, Narvahan. Had I not given birth to a boy, what would have happened then? I would have lost my place in everyone's heart. Sometimes I wonder what is a woman for? I am unable to understand. Is she only for her body, which men can charm their eyes with? Is she only for pleasure and her womb?'

She paused, as if she was collecting her thoughts, and said, 'You know? They have loved me only because they wanted something from me. Only one man, KshemGupt, loved me for what I am, but God took him away from me. Now, I have no man left who loves me for who I am,' her voice quivered by the end.

'That's not true, my queen. There are a lot of people who love you. They love you not because you are their queen, not because you are the mother of the heir and not because you win battles, but they just love you for who you are. Maybe you just don't realize but they are around you,' a woeful Nirvahana commiserated his thought. Amidst all the bloodshed and turmoil in the kingdom, Narvahan himself didn't realize when his admiration for Didda secretly blossomed into love.

'But what should I do, Narvahan? I can't take this anymore.'

'As you said, my queen, Shiva is incomplete without Shakti and Shakti is also incomplete without Shiva. You need a Shiva to make you complete. I know you have shown the world that a woman alone can be a great strength. You have proved that she needs no one to take care of her. But, my queen, we all need someone to fill the void inside us. You need a companion to be with you, for you, to be the love that you have always wanted, to stop your enemies from plotting to win over you and your kingdom…' Didda interrupted him and asked, 'By the way, have you made the preparations for the court meeting tomorrow?'

'Y...Yes,' Narvahan said abruptly.

Didda could sense something was not quite right from her conversation with Narvahan. That was why she changed the topic and asked Narvahan to leave shortly after. It was not difficult for Didda to understand what Narvahan meant when he exemplified Shiva and Shakti. Didda was restless after the conversation. She was disturbed and worried and called Valaga to assuage her doubts.

'What has happened to you? A victorious queen should not have a worried face,' said Valaga.

'Nothing has happened; I am fine!'

'You know you cannot hide anything from me, Didda. Tell me what has happened.'

'Narvahan. I think he has led himself on to a wrong path, Valaga. I am afraid I will have to stop him.'

'What has happened to him?'

'He said something that I had never expected from him,' said Didda.

Valaga responded with a subtle smile, 'I know what he might have said.'

'No, you don't, Valaga. He said that I need someone besides me to complete me. What I sensed in his eyes was unimaginable. No man on this earth can see a woman as just a woman. They always want something more. There is always an expectation; everyone has a motive, even Narvahan.'

'What's wrong with what he has said. I could sense his feelings from the very first time we met. Tell me Didda, who has been your sole supporter when no one was around? Who

Narvahan's Death and the End of an Era 135

has been there in all your struggles? Who had taken you to AbhinavGupt and saved your pride? Who had been there to support you when everyone in the palace and the court was plotting against you? It was only one person. It was Narvahan,' said Valaga.

'So, if he too has done all of this for a purpose, then what's the difference? I believed he is just an honest courtier, a wise minister and a loyal friend. He means a lot to me, but he wants to take the place of KshemGupt. How can I give him that place? I vowed my life for my king in front of Lord Shiva. No one can take his place.'

'So, don't give him that place. That's up to you. But make sure that you don't lose him because of this. He is the most valuable person in your life at the moment.'

'I know, Valaga, but I cannot forget what he feels for me. I cannot be the same around him for now I know the truth. I feel betrayed, Valaga.'

'What can I say on this? He has hidden his feeling for so long because he did not want you to feel this way. But, destiny wanted this to be revealed. I suggest you accept it and move on. I know you are wise enough to take care of this.'

Valaga left the room, expecting Didda to take the right decision. Narvahan's words tormented Didda. She also felt that Valaga, who had been there for Didda since her childhood, had also changed sides. The wheel of fate had begun to turn one more time.

'All could never be well in Didda's time,' as the wise men would often say. Troubled and restless, Didda retired to her chamber in a pensive mood.

Narvahan paced up and down in his chamber; he could

sense that he had lost the faith that Didda had in him. He wanted to restore Didda's confidence, not just in him but all that he stood for. Narvahan mustered the courage for one last battle of integrity that he knew he must fight for himself. He rushed to his desk and took out a parchment laced with musk, meant for very special occasions, and began to write. Narvahan spent two prahars filling the parchment with resolute words. He wanted to ensure that Didda understood him and perhaps gave him a chance to redeem himself. Satisfied, he summoned the sewak and sent the letter to Didda.

Valaga received the letter. She went to Didda with Narvahan's parchment and sat beside her. Valaga told Didda, 'Narvahan has sent a letter for you and you must read it. Narvahan deserves a chance.'

'Letter? Read it aloud, Valaga,' Didda commanded. She somehow had a bad feeling about it.

Valaga not only read Didda's mind, she also saw a surge of emotions splattering across her beautiful face. Didda had never been good at hiding extreme emotions from Valaga.

'You must give him a chance,' said Valaga softly.

'What does he want? First, read what he has written,' Didda almost snapped at Valaga. Anxiety had paved way for anger and Valaga knew that Didda had almost made up her mind.

'Narvahan has requested you to honour him by accepting to have a meal with him.' Valaga was soft in her words. She spoke almost pleading on behalf of Narvahan. Didda remained quiet, battling her own turmoil; perhaps she was still trying to reason with Narvahan's fall from grace.

It was just the beginning of a long wait and Narvahan paced across his chamber. His heart pounded against his chest as he went through each and every word that he wrote. His mind was vacillating... 'Will Didda let his slip pass, or will she remain by her resolute demeanor? Will she, won't she'...and the night slowly passed by as the longest ever for Narvahan who didn't catch a wink. As the sun rose from across the Pir Panjal Mountains, Narvahan felt somnolent.

Valaga entered Narvahn's chamber. He had fallen asleep on the desk. She walked up to him and looked at the face of a man distraught by love. Valaga felt a sudden bout of melancholy. 'Here lies a beaten man who just before dusk was a glorious warrior and an extraordinary minister, someone who was the cornerstone of Kashmir's resurgence.'

Valaga gently touched his shoulder, hard enough to wake him up. Narvahan jolted from his short slumber and was surprised to see Valaga in his chamber.

'I have a message from the queen,' Valaga spoke, wanting to get over with the conversation as quickly as she could. She didn't have the heart to face Narvahan for long.

'Queen? Ah, Didda...yes Valaga, what time is she coming?' asked an eager Narvahan while getting up from his desk and rearranging his attire.

'I am sorry, but she has declined, of course, due to pressing engagements of the court,' replied Valaga. Valaga saw a crestfallen man in front of him. 'I must leave now as the queen has to attend the court,' said Valaga and quickly moved out of Narvahan's chamber.

That morning, Didda had asked the court to meet. Narvahan came to discuss the agenda for the meeting, as he usually did, but he was told by Didda's chambermaid that she would meet him directly in the court.

The atmosphere in the court felt different. Even though Narvahan sat right next to the queen, the distance between them felt at apogees. Didda did not even look at him with a smile like she always did. Her eyes today were not searching for Narvahan, like they always did before every decision.

Then, when the court discussed and suggested that Minister Dhrupad, the manager of public grievances in the court, should be given the responsibility to govern the newly-won land, Narvahan protested vehemently, 'His record is not hidden from anyone, my queen. Dhrupad is corrupt and a shrewd minister. He, for long, had his allegiance to Phalgun and indulged in many ploys against you and the kingdom. I request you not to consider him for such a huge responsibility.'

'Mind your decorum when you speak in this court, Narvahan. Speak only when you are asked to. Do not intervene when the queen is addressing the court. You know I can punish you for this indiscipline, but for now, I just order you to leave my court,' said the stringent queen.

Narvahan could not believe what he had just heard. Didda, who always considered him as her backbone, had asked him, Narvahan, who had dedicated his every breath to her, to leave the court. She had disrespected him in front of the whole court. How could she do that? Narvahan was shattered. He could not understand why that happened. Why would Didda do that to him? He thought for a long time, and then, the whole conversation with Didda rewound in his mind. Narvahan cursed himself.

'How could I do this? How could I not stop myself? Why did I say all that to her? I have broken her trust. I have broken her heart,' Narvahan spoke to himself aloud, 'It is too much

Narvahan's Death and the End of an Era

for a servant to ask for. I should not have done this. Why did I not understand that I am just a servant. A queen cannot love me. I have ruined everything. Now, she will never see me the way she used to. I have lost Didda. I have lost my respect. I have lost my pride. I have lost everything.'

Narvahan was stupefied. His heart was pounding. At that very moment, without any second thoughts, he took out his dagger and pierced his heart with it. His scream echoed across the same corridors that stood witness to the rise and fall of Narvahan.

There was pandemonium and the pradhan sewak ran towards the court, which was still in session. He informed the court that Narvahan had killed himself. For that one moment, Didda's entire life from the time she had wed and come to Kashmir flashed in front of her eyes. She felt responsible for his death. She sunk into deep sorrow and the entire court was stunned.

Didda could not believe this. She tried but could not move from her throne. She took a moment and then blinked her eyes to hide her tears. She quickly went to her room and broke down in the privacy of her chamber. She suddenly felt a void in her life. 'What have I done? I should not have done this. I have *killed* Narvahan. I am responsible for his death.' Didda cried in Valaga's embrace.

'You cannot write anyone's fate, Didda. It is destiny. Don't blame yourself and accept what has happened.' Valaga consoled Didda stoically.

For many days, Didda was remorseful with guilt. She had never expected a man of valour and glory to go down so meekly into oblivion. Maybe she had expected him to show greater resolute in his feelings towards her. Didda wasn't sure of her conflict. Even in his death, Narvahan had made Didda stronger for the times ahead.

'Why should I cry for him? I never loved him. I respected him as a minister. I adored him as a friend, but I never lied to him. He should have respected my feelings. How could I give anyone the place that I had given to my beloved king? If he could not accept this and left me for not loving him, then he was too selfish. He also wanted something from a woman like everybody else. Some want your body, some want your beauty, some want your fertility, and some want your heart. There is no one who can love a woman without a desire. But I am not a commodity. I am a woman and I need no one beside me to be complete. I am complete myself. I am strong enough to fight my challenges alone. I am stronger than the man who could not accept a women's rejection.'

That day onwards, she believed that the only reason for Narvahan's death was Narvahan himself. His death was not a sacrifice for either himself or for Didda. Soon, Didda began to attend the court as before.

Abhimanyu had begun to learn his lessons in statesmanship and administration under Didda's wings. There were times she felt if Narvahan had groomed Abhimanyu, he wouldn't have been so weak.

Soon, Abhimanyu started managing the kingdom and Didda believed that it was her calling to renounce the world and become a monk. But before she did that, Didda wanted to complete one last task. She wanted Abhimanyu to get married and ensure that a proper succession plan was in place. She wanted neither another Chandralekha nor another Didda to be born. She did not want Abhimanyu to endure what KshemGupt did. There was a fear hidden deep inside her—the curse of SangramDev. 'Had it waned? Or was it still looming over her progeny?' she often wondered.

There was also something odd about Abhimanyu that bothered Didda. It was not that Abhimanyu was his father's reflection; Didda knew he won't ever be as debauched as King KshemGupt had been before meeting her. But still, there was something else that often made Didda restless. Abhimanyu was reticent and delicate. Didda often discussed this with Valaga. She was always conscious of the fact that a king needed to be his own master; perhaps Abhimanyu still had a long way to go to become what she wanted him to become.

8

Didda and the Bride from Himavat

It was fascinating how Didda had managed the kingdom after KshemGupt's death. She had even managed to carve a name for herself amongst the most famous and courageous warriors.

She had proved all those wrong who believed in the notion that a woman cannot rule a kingdom. It was nothing but her own mettle that made her victorious.

By now, the masses could not stop singing praises in the name of Didda. Her name commanded respect for Kashmir and herself. The prince of this prosperous kingdom was also drawing attention. Every king wanted to marry their daughter into the kingdom and forge new ties with this powerful ruler.

Everyone realized the importance of being Didda's daughter-in-law. It was incredible how the times had changed. From being an unwanted girl to the most sought-after queen—Didda had truly come of age. Everyone believed they knew what Didda would seek in her daughter-in-law, however, Didda just wanted what she could never become.

कार्येषु मन्त्री करणेषु दासी, भोज्येषु माता शयनेषु रम्भा ।
धर्मानुकूला क्षमया धरित्री, भार्या च षाड्गुण्यवतीह दुर्लभा

(A wife at work should be an advisor; in adherence,
a server; a mother while serving food; in affection,
Rambha; an expert in religion and laws and an epitome
of forgiveness.)

These six qualities were essential in those days and Didda too, first and foremost, desired these qualities in her daughter-in-law. Kings and rulers everywhere knew that more than becoming a wife to the king, any girl marrying him would first become the daughter-in-law of Queen Didda. And this was the most coveted fact for them. If Didda chose a princess, it would be a proud moment for that kingdom. It would prove that their daughter had the best upbringing amongst all. In fact, many kings had already started teaching their daughters the art of warfare in case Didda enquired about their combat skills or horse riding.

Didda decided to speak to Abhimanyu if he had something on his mind as his wife. Abhimanyu left this decision to his mother as he firmly believed that she could never go wrong. However, when the moment came to pick a princess for her son, Didda rejected all those who were trained in warfare.

Valaga was curious to know the reason behind her decision. 'I know King Abhimanyu may not be the best-learned man around, but when the time would come, he will be an able ruler and defend his kingdom,' Didda replied.

'I do not understand, Didda,' Valaga continued.

'Children always have traces of their ancestor's courage. Abhimanyu's grandfather had revolted against the meandering king and ruled over Kashmir. He was courageous, and I believe Abhimanyu has those qualities as well,' Didda explained.

Didda knew that as long as she was alive, Kashmir was

safe from all dangers. Therefore, she desired a companion for Abhimanyu and not a warrior. All Didda wanted was a simple girl who would look after her son and respect him. She wanted an end to all the bloodshed and treachery. Deep inside, she was hoping and praying for the curse of SangramDev to have taken its fill.

Didda ensured that her son's wedding had no political connotations. She neither wanted any riches nor did she desire any traditions to be followed. The only thing that mattered to her was the blessings of AbhinavGupt. Abhimanyu was free to make his own choice with regards to his wife and that is why Didda decided to organize a huge ceremony for him to be able to choose his wife best-suited to his disposition—a *swayamvaram*.

All the princesses present were more enthusiastic to become Didda's daughter-in-law than Abhimanyu's wife.

In that crowd of princesses, Didda noticed AdityaRaj, the king of Himavat with his daughter Vasundhara. AdityaRaj, upon his arrival, had discovered that the other princesses were talented and skilled in different areas and art forms. He thought then that it was best for him to abjure since his daughter was just a naive princess raised with an upbringing that marriage was a princess's ultimate purpose in life. Didda would never prefer such a simple girl. However, Didda had not failed to notice that Vasundhara was drawn to Abhimanyu. Her eyes were constantly gazing at Abhimanyu and the ceremonies were of least interest to her. Didda could see the love for her son in her eyes. Love was Didda's only weakness. It was love that she wanted for her son.

Vasundhara's eyes constantly reminded Didda of someone, but she couldn't place who exactly. Just then, AdityaRaj turned to his daughter and said, 'Your destiny does not lie here.' As soon as Vasundhara heard this, she turned her glance away and started to leave the palace. She did not even turn back once to look at Abhimanyu. Her father's instructions were binding, and she left behind the man she had begun falling in love with. Vasundhara indeed was an ideal daughter.

Her departure was troubling Didda. She wanted Vasundhara to stop her father; she wanted her to say that she will participate in the swayamvaram. But she did not do any such thing. She quietly walked away, following her father, but Didda knew what was going inside her mind and heart. Didda recalled how years ago, she had been a mute witness to a somewhat-similar sacrifice made by a daughter for her father. Didda had chosen to be silent then because she had to save her son's life.

At that moment, Didda realized that Vasundhara reminded her of Chandralekha, her innocent eyes, the dedication towards her father, and eventually, her death on KshemGupt's pyre. Didda was a witness when Chandralekha walked into the flames for her father. The same flames still burnt inside her heart and history was about to repeat itself.

She stopped AdityaRaj and welcomed his daughter with a lot of affection. King AdityaRaj was confused with what was happening until Didda stood up and made a formal public announcement about Abhimanyu and Vasundhara's wedding. Everyone was surprised by the choice Didda had made.

Their marriage was solemnized with grandeur and ostentation. Kashmir was abuzz with high expectations and people believed that the new queen would take Kashmir to even greater heights. Little did anyone know that the new bride was incomparable to Queen Didda.

Vasundhara could read the physiognomy on everyone's faces. She felt just one uneasy message ringing in her ears all the time that 'she was not good enough' for Abhimanyu and the queen had obliged her by choosing her for her son. She kept wondering why did Didda choose her over so many capable brides?

Destiny had begun testing Vasundhara's innocence. She was just a simple princess who was here to set up a whole new world with the prince, but she failed to understand why the people were so contemptuous of her. She had no idea that she was being compared to Didda in every aspect. When people called her fortunate, she felt they were mocking her, making her realize that she did not deserve this place. However, she had no one to share her thoughts with. She was scared that her own identity was being dwarfed by comparisons to Didda. She only hoped that her husband would not see her in the same light as others.

Vasundhara was lucky. Abhimanyu neither had siblings nor any friends or relatives. After KshemGupt's sudden death, a fear of losing his life and Kashmir as prematurely as his father did lurk in his mind. There had been many attempts on his life, but Didda had managed to save him every time. Didda had always kept Abhimanyu under a strict vigil and it was to this apprehension that he lost his childhood. He had not lived freely till now. Even though Didda had him trained by VikramSen to become an excellent warrior, he was entirely dependent on her. He had a strong belief that as long as Didda was alive he would not come in harm's way.

In Vasundhara, he found a companion; someone who was born just for him. They were almost of the same age,

Didda and the Bride from Himavat 147

but Vasundhara was more of an extrovert. She never sought permission before venturing into any activity. In her father's kingdom, her suggestion became the rule. AdityaRaj had brought her up with a lot of love and she had never known any fear. Nothing weighed down her spirits. She could do what she pleased, and roaming happily around the entire kingdom with her friends was her favourite pastime.

King AdityaRaj's small kingdom was situated somewhere between Tibet and Kashmir, amidst tall overarching mountains. It had never faced any conquests, thus, there was never a need to tighten security. Vasudhara's outgoing nature was the result of such an environment. But, after her wedding, she found herself in a completely contrasting environment at her in-laws' abode.

Vasundhara was upset about the fact that her husband had an unseated fear gnawing inside him, which had restrained Abhimanyu from experiencing the adventures of a normal childhood. She thought this was unfair. She grappled with the guards to go from one room to the other. That stifled her, and she often asked the guards, 'If someone wanted to reach me, would they be able to?' But Abhimanyu did not know how does one live otherwise. There was a constant question in her head, 'Is this living life to the fullest?'

She did not know that when Didda had married KshemGupt Kashmir had been decaying and on the verge of disintegration. It had been Didda's constant efforts and perseverance that had brought Kashmir to where it was then. Thousands had sacrificed their lives because they believed in Didda and her conviction that Kashmir could be a prosperous kingdom. Since a woman could not rule, she had faced a lot of protest and criticism. It was only after she gave a prince to the throne that she won the support of the masses, with which she turned Kashmir into a full-fledged dynasty. Abhimanyu was not just a king but also the epitome of strength and benevolence for lakhs of Kashmiris. His security was Didda's prime concern.

Abhimanyu would have to lead an insular, protected life until the time he could have his own sons. Once he did, he could probably free himself from the limitation he then faced. However, Vasundhara was too young to understand those intricacies.

Abhimanyu found himself immensely attracted to Vasundhara and her independent ways. Vasundhara would rile him with the sense of freedom she had enjoyed in her father's kingdom. Little did Abhimanyu realize that the innocent unassuming Vasundhara was unintentionally sowing the seeds of revolution in his mind. Young and full of energy, she had already broken a few rules of the palace laid down by Didda. It began with Abhimanyu standing in his balcony which Didda felt would expose him to the enemy's marksman. Though Abhimanyu was trained, enough to defend himself, Didda did not wish to risk his life.

Vasundhara, on the other hand, believed that if Abhimanyu was not safe in his own land, where else could he be safe! It was her firm belief that rather than restricting Abhimanyu from standing in the balcony, the security within the kingdom needed to be improved.

Vasundhara was naive for she did not know the fickleness of the human mind. Nobody could comprehend when someone would change their mind and decide to retaliate or attack. Didda firmly believed that not even wild animals had as much hatred and poison in them as humans did in their minds. That is why she ensured that the security of King Abhimanyu was changed at regular intervals.

Vasundhara was full of youthful enthusiasm and ignorant of the convolutions of a human mind. She was too young to have this wisdom. Vasundhara would often insist on Abhimanyu to stand in the balcony with her and look at the moon beaming its beautiful light on the river Vitasta flowing below. She wanted Abhimanyu to be by her side while admiring the beauty around. Abhimanyu, consumed by her mystic amour, felt helpless. She often took him from one part of the palace to another, surreptitiously escaping the furtive eyes of the royal guards, just to prove to Abhimanyu that all was safe. They sometimes escaped to the banks of Vitasta and looked at the stars floating away on the serene river. Abhimanyu started to enjoy his newfound covert freedom.

He had started to open up; people could now tell from his body mannerisms that this alliance had come of age. His face glowed, and Vasundhara was happy too for her husband lived up to her expectations. The news spread far and wide about the regal couple and the happiness Vasundhara had brought into King Abhimanyu's life. Thus, the people of Kashmir grew fond of Queen Vasundhara.

Didda was also pleased by this. She was happy that Vasundhara had managed to earn everybody's respect. She felt this was an appropriate time for them to have a progeny, a symbol of a loving bond yielding a happy child. She wanted Abhimanyu to have many children so that the children would never have to undergo what Abhimanyu had to endure as he was a single child. She didn't want her grandchildren to be overburdened by expectations. Queen Didda remained quiet in spite of knowing that Abhimanyu and Vasundhara had transgressed many rules, for she saw the love blossoming behind these transgressions.

Since Vasundhara's intentions were noble and innocent, Didda never stopped them. She also did not let either of them know that she was aware of what they had been up to. The freedom that both experienced was safe under Didda's watchful eyes.

In fact, Didda had ensured their protection from day one. However, things started to worsen when Vasundhara wanted to visit her friends and parents in her father's kingdom, Himavat. Abhimanyu had assured her that he would arrange for her visit the next day but Vasundhara had become habitual in breaking the rules.

'Still obeying rules, are we, my king?' Vasundhara taunted Abhimanyu.

'Would it not be an amazing adventure to leave without telling anyone?' she continued.

Abhimanyu eventually relented. They thought they could reach Himavat overnight.

Their security forces shadowed them in disguise till the borders of Kashmir but when they saw them leaving the kingdom, they came forth and confronted them. Abhimanyu was their king and so he asked all his security to return immediately. However, they refused to say that it was Didda's orders to stay by him and not allow them to leave the kingdom's borders.

Vasundhara was enraged and ordered them to leave as their queen. However, these were soldiers of Kashmir with sworn allegiance to none other than Didda. They brought both of them back forcefully. Vasundhara felt offended, humiliated and something churned inside her. Abhimanyu, on the other hand, felt proud of Didda for he had just witnessed how efficiently his mother managed the kingdom.

Vasundhara felt like a prisoner in her own kingdom. She felt that she was not a queen, not in the true sense, but only a namesake. The real queen was still Didda. Vasundhara felt helpless and worthless to be the wife of a king who had no authority at all. What was worse for her was that he didn't seem to mind.

Destiny played its part and the wheel turned, once more. All this while, she thought that she had taught her husband how to live a fuller life, but she now realized that she was mistaken. She understood that since the soldiers were shadowing them, Didda had always known of all those adventures. Her juvenile self was deeply distressed at the thought of being married to naught.

She found herself soaked in vengeance and she unknowingly began her descent onto a path that would devastate lives and alter the course of history.

'Who actually runs the palace? Does the king only obey his mother's instructions? But then, what kind of king is Abhimanyu? The one who cannot even take his own decisions?' Many questions smouldered inside Vasundhara.

A few days later, Vasundhara expressed her desire to be a part of the royal proceedings at the court. She had seen her father rule and now she wanted to test her husband. What she saw confirmed her worst fears. She saw Didda in the court and realized she was nothing compared to the warrior queen.

She was not her usual happy self now. She was upset most

of the time and considered herself a prisoner like her husband. After some thought, she decided to sideline Didda and make sure her husband was proven as the rightful king. She conspired against Didda and thought of ways to send her away. Vasundhara now sought retribution.

In her dark rage, she heard of her father's arrival in Srinagaram. It was an overwhelming feeling for Vasundhara. The father-daughter reunited after a long time. Didda, however, knew that Tibet had brought Himavat to Kashmir not the love for his daughter. Tibet was a prosperous kingdom and an important trade route between Kashmir and the great Asian plains. AdityaRaj desired to rule over it. However, he could not do it without strategic military support from Kashmir.

That night, Vasundhara sought a promise from her husband to support her father in anything that he pursued. She explained that he was the king and it was his responsibility to help AdityaRaj. However, Abhimanyu maintained that his mother took all such decisions. If Didda deemed necessary then she would, without a doubt, support his father-in-law.

Vasundhara could not contain her emotions any longer. For many days, her anger had been simmering yet repressed within herself. She questioned Abhimanyu if he or Didda was the ruler, and if she said no, would he not help her father.

That night witnessed an intense discussion between Abhimanyu and Vasundhara. She felt that Didda was treated like a goddess, and nothing else within the royal walls mattered more than her words. Abhimanyu was perturbed seeing his wife so upset. He promised to help AdityaRaj.

The following day, AdityaRaj proposed to attack Tibet. It had been a sovereign kingdom and an old ally to Kashmir,

Didda and the Bride from Himavat 153

but of late, Tibet had become a conduit to Islamic warlords. Abhimanyu immediately agreed to support him.

In the event of an invasion, Tibet could create complications for Kashmir. Didda was not surprised when Abhimanyu spoke in favour without waiting for Didda's consent. The court was receptive that the king was in favour of helping his relatives. However, they also noticed that Didda remained silent and indubitably stated that they would only cast their votes once they hear Didda's opinion on this matter.

Vasundhara had anticipated that Didda would support her son in this decision but she refused. Vasundhara was extremely upset. She took this as an insult of her husband and father. Abhimanyu, on the other hand, was unable to look the courtiers in the eyes. Didda looked around and observed everybody's expressions. She then spoke. She shared that Tibet had been a powerful old ally, whereas the kingdom of AdityaRaj was a recent addition. She could not risk losing an old relationship in the hands of a new one. Hearing Didda, the royal court supported her plea. King AdityaRaj, thus, returned empty-handed and this infuriated Vasundhara more. Her hatred and animosity for Didda fostered as she walked out of the court in anger.

She stopped talking to Abhimanyu and gave up food. She was now adamant on going back to her father. This worsened her health and when the royal physician arrived to check on her, the news of her pregnancy broke.

The happiness of Abhimanyu and Didda knew no limits. The entire kingdom of Kashmir was joyous and immersed in celebrations. Vasundhara, however, continued to stay upset. Security around her had increased and she left like a prisoner.

She had always enjoyed her freedom and this intense security stifled her. Didda and Abhimanyu tried their best to cheer her up, but they were unsuccessful.

She could not come to terms with the fact that Didda had not kept her son's word to support and protect her father in his conquest of Tibet. She held Didda responsible for leaving her father helpless on the battlefield, despite being a close relative.

Didda knew the reason for her daughter-in-law's angst, but she had never let her personal issues overpower her decisions for her kingdom. Didda tried her best to keep things amenable between Vasundhara and her, but realized soon enough that every time they met, Vasundhara resented her. She did not even want to look at Didda. She still hoped that things would improve eventually; however, she gave up on her efforts to reconcile with Vasundhara. Didda wanted to ensure that Vasundhara's inner conflict should not affect her baby so she stopped visiting her altogether. Abhimanyu also had been granted leave from the affairs of the court, to take complete care of his wife. At Didda's behest, the royal physicians would urge the couple to indulge in walks on the esplanade across Vitasta, under the subtle watch of the royal guards. Vasundhara was well aware that they were being watched and that added to her acrimony.

Amidst her inner turmoil, Vasundhara came to know of Tibet's plan to attack Himavat. This time, Syrian warlords supported Tibet. Vasundhara was deeply concerned and worried about the welfare of her father and his kingdom. She continued to request Abhimanyu to support her father in these troubling times, but he had been unable to gather the courage to contest his mother's decision. He tried his best to convince Vasundhara that Tibet would not attack Himavat. However, this effort went futile and he was sorely disappointed when the news arrived that Tibet had attacked Himavat.

Vasundhara's father was on the battlefield while she prepared for her baby's arrival, writhing in pain. For two days, Vasundhara fought her pain. The auspicious birth of her son was marked with the news of King AdityaRaj's victory over Tibet.

With this win under his belt, the king of Himavat had made a place for himself amongst the most celebrated and courageous names. Vasundhara believed that her father's victory coinciding with her son's birth was a celestial sign.

Vasundhara's happiness knew no bounds, she had not been so happy in many months. Though she was filled with joy, her bitterness and animosity towards Didda increased in equal measures. Vasundhara's respect within the palace and kingdom had increased manifold. She had given birth to a prince and an heir to the kingdom of Kashmir. Didda was relieved that with the arrival of the little prince, Abhimanyu would finally be able to lead a commanding life.

However, Vasundhara did not trust Didda. Her dislike for Didda had begun to impair her judgment to the extent that she began to believe that Didda in her greed for power would sacrifice her son's life.

Perturbed, Vasundhara requested to call upon Mahamardan, her father's army chief, to become the guardian of her son. She did not want her son's childhood to be ruined like that of her husband's.

When the court heard of this imprudent demand, they were offended. How could Himavat's army chief become the guardian of Kashmir's prince? However, Didda surprised everyone with her consent. The courtiers realized it was not the queen's decision but that of a mother who had known the bitter taste of insecurity when Abhimanyu's life was in grave danger. She said, 'Vasundhara is, after all, a mother and every mother has the right to decide what would ensure her child's safety.' She added, 'You should all be happy that the heir's safety was being ensured by both the kingdoms.'

The court respected Didda's thoughts and Vasundhara felt belittled yet again.

Didda's consent flummoxed Vasundhara as she began to wonder why Didda supported her going against the whole court. 'What did she want after all?' With every passing day, Vasundhara began to sink into a stygian pit of hatred and an unknown fear for her son. She began to believe that Didda would eventually kill her son.

Meekly though, Vasundhara shared her fears about her son's life with Abhimanyu. AdityaRaj's victory had also made Abhimanyu confident. He loved his wife even more with AdityaRaj's victory; he began to trust her increasingly.

Abhimanyu, too, began to feel that his mother did not give him the power to act like the king he was. Didda's decision against him on the previous occasion had left him bruised as well. But what he did not realize was that Didda's decisions were because of his inability to act independently. Vasundhara also expressed her apprehensions on Didda's intent to allow Mahamardan inside the palace for protection of the prince.

Vengeance and poison have no religion, caste or creed. They seep into anyone who beckons them. Abhimanyu was no exception as he began to drift away from what once was his fortress of strength and safety.

After his father's win over Tibet, Vasundhara began to

believe that he was a match to Didda in terms of valour and legacy. Vasundhara was beyond reason and began to hatch the nefarious conspiracy that would have AdityaRaj depose off Didda. Didda was well aware of what had been on Vasundhara's mind. She found her at the same crossroads that she once had been. Didn't Didda too love her husband and did everything in her power to protect him and her son? She could see the same love in Vasundhara's heart for Abhimanyu; she was a little imprudent though. Deep inside, Didda prayed, that Vasundhara would realign herself.

Didda began to contemplate; 'Would Vasundhara be able to manage the kingdom the same way she had by keeping the king in the forefront?' She was appreciative of Vasundhara's decision to have AdityaRaj's security forces guard the little prince. She knew that if this girl had the capability and courage to go against her, the much-revered queen's decisions to ensure her son's safety, she was capable of a lot more.

It was evident to everyone that Vasundhara was going against Didda, and whispers of their growing difference disseminated the kingdom. However, Didda was not perturbed for she knew that this concurrence would lead to the emergence of a new female leadership. Didda understood that her son was not worthy of taking over her responsibilities and she wanted to test if Vasundhara could manage to run and rule over the affairs of the kingdom as she had. Didda also knew that Vasundhara was not ready at the moment and needed to learn a lot before she could even think of putting her through this.

If by accepting Vasundhara the way she was, Didda could make her ready for the throne, this effort would not be a fallacious proposition. She knew that Vasundhara would be able to cope with almost everything for the sake of her kingdom. Blazoned with this possibility, Didda sent for VikramSen, yet again, and this time to train Vasundhara. The throne of Srinagaram was to prepare for yet another queen. Didda had decided to anoint Vasundhara as the regent.

'I am not through with you yet,' destiny seemed to whisper into Didda's ears.

A few days later, the royal physician informed Didda that the little prince was physically weak, and his growth was not as anticipated. He told her that the prince might have an impaired growth. For the first time, Didda was scared, not for the throne but of a mother's anger. She saw Destiny mocking her. The torment and wrath of Vasundhara would gather wind which would soon besiege her doors.

At this time of unrest, she could only think of AbhinavGupt.

'I can't take this anymore. How long do I have to endure,' she pleaded with him.

'Till destiny has nothing more to offer,' AbhinavGupt smiled.

Didda limped back to the palace, hoping her fears would dissipate. Throughout the night, she could hear the guffaws of SangramDev—his curse had not waned.

The next day, she went to Vasundhara's chambers after a long time, to see her grandson. The news of her arrival perturbed Vasundhara and her heart began to beat fast.

'Didda was a bad omen,' her mind repeated. She was anxious that there must be some bad news, else why would Didda, who had only visited the prince when he was born, come to see him suddenly?

Didda entered the chamber and picked up the little prince

Didda and the Bride from Himavat 159

in her arms. She knew what Vasundhara was thinking but she also knew that only a mother could understand and share the pain of another.

It was not easy for Didda to break the news. It was more difficult than accepting she was ominous.

Vasundhara's fears took on a demonic shape. She felt her heart being pierced and lost consciousness. She woke up to see the royal physicians attending her. They also informed her that different formulations were being developed for the prince to aid his growth and strength.

Didda too arrived and she advised Vasundhara that a mother's mental health affects her child's well-being. She told her to concentrate on her son's health and nothing else.

'Leave all your worries to me, I will take care of everything else,' Didda said emphatically, trying to verve Vasundhara.

But, Vasundhara was no longer a mother; she was a woman consumed by rage, vengeance and hatred for everything and everyone.

'Didda has consumed your son,' she heard her dark soul whisper.

'Leave everything to me'—Didda's words echoed in her mind.

Vasundhara was losing herself and she advised Abhimanyu against taking the royal physicians' help.

'Leave everything to me'—she just could not get those words out of her mind. She was certain that Didda had planned to exterminate her son.

Abhimanyu, however, was still unsure of her fears.

'Mother will never harm her own,' said Abhimanyu.

'She will kill my son and then get you married to someone

else,' Vasundhara sobbed inconsolably.

Abhimanyu was stuck in this flurry of thoughts. He knew that Didda did not consider him efficient enough for the throne at the moment, but would she plot against his little son? Vasundhara was apprehensive of Abhimanyu's stance. She wanted Abhimanyu to believe that Didda just wanted an heir for namesake. In reality, she wanted to keep the reigns of the kingdom in her hands. She belaboured him with dissimulated facts about how Didda had fooled his father in the name of love and married him; how she had separated Phalgun from him and manipulated with Narvahan to stage the murder of Chandralekha; how she had chased out KshemGupt's nephews out of their own kingdom.

Abhimanyu still was in no mood to believe his wife and seemed petulant. He dismissed Vasundhara and her ideas as just a figment of her imagination. He was sure Didda had no such intentions. Vasundhara was adamant. She said Didda had chosen her to be his wife only because she did not want anyone stronger than her to be her daughter-in-law. How else would she be able to retain her authority and rule?

'If you won't do anything to save your own son, then I will do whatever I deem necessary to protect him. You have to decide if you want to remain with your hands tied behind your back or do something for your family,' she howled.

Abhimanyu was nonplussed. According to his wife, his mother only wanted to rule, but if his mother only wanted the throne and power, then what did his wife want? He could not help but ask Vasundhara if she wanted the throne for herself.

Abhimanyu took his little prince in his arms and said that they would need to leave for Himavat immediately.

Didda and the Bride from Himavat 161

All three—Vasundhara, Abhimanyu and NandiGupt, the little prince—reached Didda's room. Abhimanyu said, 'I have no interest in this throne, this power or any of these material things. You keep your throne, we are renouncing this royal life and going away.'

Didda heard him clearly but continued to remain seated and seemed unperturbed. Valaga wanted to ask why they were leaving but Didda stopped her. She then turned to Vasundhara and Abhimanyu and said, 'Alright, you can leave if you wish to.'

Neither did she ask them anything nor did she attempt to stop them. Abhimanyu and Vasundhara were shocked.

'What kind of a mother is she?' they both thought.

An enraged Vasundhara lost all patience. She turned towards Abhimanyu and said, 'At least now do you believe that your mother is a witch? The throne of Kashmir and the power that comes with it are her sole concerns. She doesn't even care if we stay or leave. You did not believe me, but now you have seen for yourself.'

Then, she turned to Didda and continued, 'You should leave the kingdom and not us as we are the rightful heirs to the throne. Abhimanyu and his son are the rightful kings. If someone needs to leave the kingdom, it's you and not us.'

She addressed Abhimanyu, 'If need be, I will summon my father and he will descend on her like fury. It is time you decide what you want to do with your mother.'

Vasundhara marched back to her chambers with a defeated son following in her wake.

Whatever happened was far beyond Abhimanyu's comprehension. In those moments, he felt overwhelming grief for having lost his mother. He not only felt orphaned but also cheated of his mother's love. His grief eventually paved way for rage and he ordered Mahamardan to oust Didda from the palace.

Valaga, on the other hand, was unable to understand why Didda was quiet. She began convincing Didda to take control of the situation before it deteriorated further. Didda simply said, 'I always tried convincing myself that my son was capable of ruling wisely, but today he proved me wrong. It is on his shoulders that the kingdom rests and if a king can be so bereft of his responsibilities then, he was always unworthy of the crown. He did not even think once that his decision would leave the kingdom and his people in a complete lurch. Lives and economy both would be ruined. Being swayed by emotions is not the virtue of the king of Kashmir. Even if he did want to leave, he should have deputized someone to take over his responsibilities while he was away. But he did none of that. Instead, he just came and announced his decision arbitrarily to leave without thinking of the consequences. His presence or absence, therefore, is of no value to the kingdom and I was left with no reason to stop him,' said a resolute Didda.

'But, he is also your son; you should have asked him as a mother,' Valaga intervened.

'These days he does not understand his mother. If he did, he would know that the constant watch over him was only for his safety. I had high hopes from his wife, but even she walked out with him. It was her duty to explain the difference between right and wrong, and not support him in wrong decisions. She should have understood that my son is not mature enough to take his own decisions and that is why I must intervene every time. If this means I am to be misunderstood, so be it. I will wait for my son to gain adequate wisdom to take correct decisions. I do not want to weaken him by showering him with affection. Though he may be wrong today, I am happy he has at least managed to take a decision for himself and if he survives the aftermath of this decision, I have no doubt that he will emerge as a better human being. As a mother, I have ensured more doors open up for him by not stopping him today.'

Valaga was worried about the consequences. Just then, Didda noticed the Army Chief Mahamardan leaving the palace and riding towards AdityaRaj. She also noticed the humdrum around Abhimanyu's palace along with the increase in his security cover. She looked at Valaga and said that her worries were over. Valaga did not comprehend what Didda meant and enquired further.

Didda said, 'My daughter-in-law has taken the right decision of not leaving the kingdom, if not my son.'

Soonafter, Mahamardan arrived rather early and said to her, 'It is the order of the king of Kashmir that you should leave the kingdom immediately. Failure on your part to follow his instructions will force me to take strict action against you.'

For a moment, this news disturbed Didda but seeing Mahamardan in front of her, she controlled her emotions. Although she had not expected this, she smiled and asked Mahamardan, 'Does your sword have the mettle to rise against me?'

He knew very well what Didda implied. Before he could answer, Didda turned to Valaga and said, 'Take your belongings, it is time to leave the palace.'

VikramSen also sensed something was going on in the palace. He rushed towards Didda's chambers. Valaga saw him coming and accosted him to intervene. Seeing VikramSen's imposing deposition, Mahamardan was left overwhelmed. He stood there silently. VikramSen said to Didda, 'This is your kingdom and you should not leave it.'

Didda replied, 'I have already done whatever I needed to do for this kingdom. My son, the king, does not want me to stay here anymore and hence I must honour his wishes. Anyway, I don't want to be the reason for any discord between Vasundhara and Abhimanyu. Vasundhara will rule and I will request you support her endeavours. Since you are here now, I am no longer worried about the future of Kashmir.'

VikramSen replied, 'Your leaving will disrupt the peace of the kingdom. Everything will disintegrate; your people love you. Ousting you from the kingdom may cause anger and restlessness amongst the people and there could be a potential threat to Abhimanyu's life too.'

Didda knew that he was right, but she was unable to assay and resolve this critical path. She did not want to stay in a palace when she had been instructed to leave the kingdom by her son, she had coronated not long ago. VikramSen, as the leader of the Ekangi's, authoritatively asked Mahamardan to deliver a message to his King Abhimanyu. He said, 'If your king does not want to endanger his life, ask him to take back his orders of ousting Didda from the kingdom. As far as the question of Didda's stay is concerned, she would stay amongst her people. If that is not acceptable to him, then he should leave the decision to the people—they will decide who stays in the palace and who leaves.'

Mahamardan immediately shared this message with Abhimanyu. Hearing this, Vasundhara heaved a sigh of relief.

Didda and the Bride from Himavat 165

She had extrapolated that Didda's presence within her sight was better as she would be aware of her ploys. Had she left the kingdom, she would not be able to foretell when Didda would hatch a conspiracy and attack them.

Based on this reasoning, Abhimanyu and Vasundhara took their orders back and allowed Didda to stay amongst the commoners.

Didda left the palace with a heavy heart.

As soon as Vasundhara's father heard the news, he rushed to Kashmir. He was forced to keep quiet because of his promise to Didda but he wanted to tell Abhimanyu and his daughter that the real reason behind his victory was Didda's support. He told Abhimanyu that he had committed a huge mistake by doubting someone as noble as Didda. When he came to know that the reason behind all these misdemeanours had been his own daughter, he swore never to see her as long as he lived.

Vasundhara was aggrieved by her father's decision. She had initiated this step against Didda assuming that she would have her father's unconditional support. But, after knowing her father's decision, Vasundhara was left in a quandary. After that day, neither Abhimanyu nor Vasundhara could sleep peacefully. Even though Didda had left the palace, her fear never really left them.

Abhimanyu had stopped going to the court because he feared people would question his decision. He stayed away from what his wife had always desired him to undertake. The burden of the throne weighed heavily upon him. Vasundhara was also petrified of the repercussions. She thought that Didda had left behind VikramSen on purpose, for he would exterminate her. His presence disturbed her peace of mind. She ordered him to return to his kingdom Loharin and said that she would beckon him to come, if required.

She was also paranoid that Didda would kill her son to avenge her misdeeds. So, she always stayed behind closed doors, even the rays of the sun were not permitted to reach them. Both Abhimanyu and Vasundhara were perplexed by Didda's prompt acceptance to give up her power and position and go away without any questions or resistance.

Meanwhile, Didda shared all her questions with her guru AbhinavGupt. She repeatedly asked him, 'What is my fault that everyone whom I love, eventually leaves me—my husband, my grandfather, Narvahan and now my own son who asked me to leave the palace. I have not kept him away from me even for a single day since he was born. I have no interest in power, position or this life. I want to offer myself to Shiva like my grandfather; I want to commit myself to his devotion.' Her guru listened to her patiently but remained silent.

AbhinavGupt was a spiritual master in the true sense. If he accepted someone as his disciple, he would take full responsibility for guiding them through these tempestuous moments. He heard Didda out but said nothing, except for telling her to rest.

The news of Didda's travel was proliferated in the kingdom by AbhinavGupt to prevent chaos or speculation amongst the people on not being able to see Didda regularly. Kashmir was Didda's responsibility, which was assumed by AbhinavGupt. He ensured that Didda rested well and allowed her to think freely.

This was the first time Didda displayed her sorrow. She had suppressed her emotions within her all these years. AbhinavGupt was the only one she shared her woes with.

However, her worry for Abhimanyu caused her malaise. Valaga was constantly by her side in such times, but she had also begun to grow old. AbhinavGupt himself prepared the medicines as advised by the royal physician for Didda.

A week had passed by. Didda was not used to the idea of being confined to her bed so she slowly gathered all her strength and stepped out. It seemed that it was only her body that was alive, her soul had already departed in search of KshemGupt. She had lost all her motivation to live and often questioned herself on why she was still alive. She died the day her only child had ordered her to leave the kingdom. She often worried about what she would tell KshemGupt when he would ask her about the child she gave birth to who neither respected his mother nor his kingdom. Where did she miss in imparting a good lesson to him? She often wondered.

Valaga was distressed to see her queen in this condition. She wanted to end her troubles. She had been a witness of all her miseries since her birth and felt helpless. One day, she suddenly got up and set herself on fire. Didda was alert and was able to save her. Shocked, she asked Valaga, 'Why did you do this?' Valaga replied, 'I am incapable of ending your sorrows but the least I can do is to end mine. Seeing you like this saddens me.'

AbhinavGupt explained to Didda, 'Your son's decision and attitude has pained you immensely, but you did not give up on life that very moment. Why? Because there is something that still remains.'

Didda asked, 'What is left now?'

'Life,' replied AbhinavGupt. 'Everyone has to die one day. But why wait or try for it. It will come when it has to, and we will not be able to stop or delay it. Why try for it then? Your problem lies in living this life but the day you find your renewed purpose and motivation in life, everything else will fall into place.' Didda was tentative but asked politely, 'You only explain to me what life is?'

AbhinavGupt just smiled and instructed Didda to depart for the Bhairav Nath caves the next morning. He informed her that she would find BuyaDev there. He was the in charge of the Gunj and had renounced the world. He had also accepted AbhinavGupt as his eternal guide and spiritual master. Didda would have to stay by his side and serve him.

Following her guru's orders, Didda left for the Bhairav Nath caves. After meeting BuyaDev, she immersed herself completely in his service and adhered to his every rule as instructed. BuyaDev was absorbed in his tantric meditation. Talking without any purpose was strictly prohibited. Everyone inside that cave had only one aim in life—to keep themselves engrossed in the worship of their deity.

It was not easy to understand the Advait—the philosophy of the atman and Brahma considered as one. It took ages to attain enlightenment. Didda decided to build her understanding of Advait and make it the purpose of her life based on the principles of truth.

Pratibhigya means to rise above the conscious and understand the truth and the concept of the self, to know and accept that one is not a body but a soul. Didda learnt that the reason behind everything in this universe was Shiva. BuyaDev explained, 'This earth, which is made up of multiple substances, is run as per the desires of Shiva. He can expand and collate as and when he wishes to. It is this desire of power that was often referred to as the Maheshwari power—a power that creates, facilitates survival and also destroys.'

He added, 'This meant that all human beings, the flora and fauna, rivers, including the five elements (nature, intellect, pride, ego and soul) were a part of Shiva. If all of us were the same, why was there a duality? And if there was no duality, then were we all Shiva? This is the concept of duality, about the other and self.'

He further elaborated, 'We should only search for Shiva, only then will we escape the effects of materialism and assimilate with Shiva. Sadhna, or meditation, was an effort to achieve this—which was uniting the self with Shiva. The human life had only one purpose—to escape the cycle of birth and rebirth and unite with the divine—Shiva. This is called attaining Moksha. If we simply understand this as our goal, life becomes easier.'

Didda asked, 'If we are all Shiva, then why are we so different from each other?'

BuyaDev then explained the concept of Karma. He said, 'When we are engulfed in materialism and worldly pleasures, we are bound to make choices. These choices lead us to different results. This choice is Karma. If we choose to love, what it leads us to becomes our destiny. Your destiny forms your body, your outer being. You could also choose ego, pride or a pure intent, each of these has their own results. Our mutual Karma binds us. This is like mathematics. With our good thoughts, we do good deeds for someone; the results bear fruit in the next few days, months, years or even the next birth. But it is this math of good and bad that keeps the cycle of rebirth moving. Even if you do perform good deeds, you have to be reborn to face the consequence of your good karma, and hence you end up getting separated from your Shiva.'

Didda further enquired, 'If we are born human, we will always be entangled in Karma. How do we free ourselves from it?'

BuyaDev further explained, 'If we live with the thought that everything belongs to Shiva, attaining freedom becomes easier. If we lose, we should not grieve; if we gain, we should not celebrate, because if you know Shiva, what is grief or joy to you? You have neither a parent, nor a friend, neither a child nor any material. Shiva worries for all. Why should then we worry about anything or anyone? The truth is Shiva. Materialism affects human body; even gods could not escape it. When Shiva and Sati were separated, Shiva roamed around like a crazy being. Ram would pine for Sita, but they left a good example for all of us—the human body suffers pain but to overcome this pain and not let it overpower you, and to keep your intent and action correct under difficult circumstances is life.'

Didda was convinced that this knowledge was enough for her. Thereafter, Didda only focused on Shiva. She had forgotten everything else—including her son and her kingdom. She was least affected by the outer world. She looked at humans, birds and animals with an equal eye and observed no difference. She learnt that Shiva created everything and gave them different forms according to their own Karma. Just when she was practising this knowledge, she received instructions from her guru to return, for he believed that Didda had gained all that was necessary for her to know. Didda could not refuse him.

When she stepped out of the Bhairav Nath caves, she had become a Sadhvi beaming with ojas. She started her journey on foot, limping, stumbling but yet in control. Everything inside her had transformed. Suddenly, she realized that people who were walking alongside her joined her. They looked at her scrupulously and realized it was Queen Didda indeed.

They shared the state of affairs in the kingdom. They told her that after she had left, the entire kingdom had been in a mess. Abhimanyu had not been able to handle the affairs. But, Didda remained quiet. She continued to walk and by the time she reached her guru AbhinavGupt's place, almost the entire city was walking by her side. She sought for his guidance for her next course of action. AbhinavGupt replied, 'You are already walking hand in hand with your destiny. These people need you. You need to make a choice here. Address their issues, hear out their problems and try to solve them.'

Didda accepted this as her guru's mantra. She politely enquired further, 'Where is Valaga?' The crowd spoke up, 'She is in the village. We had the honour of serving the hands that served you, our queen. How could we have missed this opportunity? She is waiting for you Queen Didda; come with us?' One of her trusted men said, from the crowd. She knew her men.

'First, I must go to my guru, AbhinavGupt,' she said and walked to his Ashram.

Didda bowed to touch her guru's feet and seek his blessings. AbhinavGupt gave her a guru mantra, 'Your personality does not need a throne or royal sanctions. If you learn to serve your people, you will be able to lead a better life. And always remember, if any action good or bad benefits the kingdom, never hesitate to take that decision. So, say the scriptures as well. Therefore, if in future, you come across such a situation, don't think twice or hesitate to do so.'

Hearing these words from her guru, Didda was wise enough to realize that destiny foresaw her becoming a Sadhvi or else she would not have had a swarm of followers.

Didda left with her trusted men. She was delighted to see that her people had nursed Valaga well. She had been looked after like a queen. Valaga was overjoyed to see Didda and asked her in a surprised tone, 'How did you reach here?' Didda replied, 'Your people brought me to your village. Will you allow me to stay with you?'

Valaga was pleased to see a transformed Didda. She bowed and asked her, 'Will you honour the villagers and me by accepting our request to stay back with us in this village?' Valaga responded to Didda's question politely and smartly.

From that day onwards, the village came to be known as ValagaMath.

People were surprised to see that Didda did not return to the palace; she did not even have the desire to do so. Instead, she expressed her desire to stay amongst Valaga's people, cross the stage of Vanashram and eventually retire from her imperial responsibilities. However, for the people of ValagaMath, the most satisfying fact was that their queen was by their side. They no longer needed any permission to see her nor would they have any security barriers restricting their access to her.

Didda was a born statesman. She mingled with the people, understanding their problems and concerns. She started to think about what she could do to help improve their lives. Various schemes were introduced, and she worked towards implementing them. Very soon, the lives of people began to change and improve.

While working there, she noticed that the women were

hard-working, dedicated and honest. She decided to enhance and empower women and this noble work began with Valaga's village. She opened the doors to education for women, as in those times, women were not formally educated. Didda strongly believed that any form of education that differentiated between genders was detrimental to the development of society. Under the help and guidance of her guru, she scouted and appointed teachers and founded a number of schools in many villages within her kingdom.

She set up medical centres for people's healthcare and made sure that medicines were easily available to all. People no longer scampered for physicians and medical assistance.

She noticed that the houses in the villages were not strong enough to withstand the harsh weather conditions. They would often get destroyed during lashing rains or extreme heat.

Didda sought the help of the workforce who had built the palace. Womenfolk in the village joined hands with them and constructed pucca houses of their own. This initiative became an example for the other villages.

The silk route passed through Kashmir those days. Didda identified local items that could be lucrative for trade and introduced them in the Eurasian market, which propelled a self-sustaining village economy.

Lodges were built for the traders and businessmen travelling between Lagur and Gujarat. These facilities also fostered trade.

Gardens were built on barren lands. She pledged to her people to participate voluntarily in strengthening the society. This made hamlets less dependent on the kingdom for their everyday needs. She established a separate village for Valaga and built a huge temple there. She had been a true friend, had stood by Didda through thick and thin and this was a heart-warming gesture from Didda. She ensured that everything in that village contributed to adding to its own beauty.

While Didda was busy in the upliftment of the society, Vasundhara was unable to believe that Didda had transformed from a sworn warrior and a queen to a monk without any territorial ambitions. Abhimanyu maximized his efforts to manage the state affairs, but he knew very well that running a state and managing a kingdom was not an easy task. Many of his decisions were fallacious and the kingdom was, thus, on uneven grounds. Many officials were corrupt and deceitful and took advantage of the naive decisions made by the king. Abhimanyu was unable to do anything despite being aware of these defilements.

He was grief-stricken and full of regret for the way he misconstrued his mother's intentions and how he had treated her. The once enchanting relationship of Abhimanyu and Vasundhara had been fading. Though he trusted her, he struggled to find reasons to continue in the same way. On the other hand, Vasundhara's father had shunned her. She could foresee that her domestic life was in danger. Abhimanyu would not speak to her for days and he would also stay away from the palace.

When Abhimanyu learnt that Didda was living peacefully in Valaga's village, he was happy for her. However, Vasundhara continued to be perturbed. She was worried that her husband would slither out of her hands. She knew that if Didda returned, he would make amends with her. Vasundhara often wondered that after her father had broken all ties with her, what would happen if her husband also ostracized her. She would be left with only Mahamardan by her side.

Didda and the Bride from Himavat 175

Meanwhile, Mahamardan began to exploit this situation for his own benefit. He had set his eyes on Kashmir. He did not want Didda back in the palace and hence he kept insinuating Vasundhara against her. He spread rumours that Didda was plotting against Vasundhara; she was living amongst the commoners and poisoning their minds against the queen. Mahamardan also contrived an attack on the prince under the pretext of protecting him. Vansundhara, who had no knowledge of traitors and conspirators, was gullible and reposed complete trust in Mahamardan.

Didda, a queen who had weathered many storms could see this conspiracy hatch within the walls of the palace, but chose to ignore it. She did not shift her focus from what she had been doing all this while. For her, her responsibility towards the people and her devotion to Shiva became primary. She only decided to obey the instructions of her guru. Didda had successfully initiated a large number of welfare mechanisms within the villages. Whether it was building dams on the Vitasta or constructing a temple, people voluntary contributed to labour and plans kept materializing even without enough funds.

Didda propagated Shaivism on a large scale as people were getting attracted to Buddhism. Didda contributed enormously in propagating Hinduism and Shaivism in Kashmir. She even facilitated the construction of many Vaishnava temples.

Didda took another important step. She chose four young Brahmins from AbhinavGupt's school, trained them and sent them to Abhimanyu as advisors for the royal court. They would be able to guide Abhimanyu on matters of the court and on what was in the best interests of the kingdom.

Abhimanyu would have to relegate from the throne if he

continued to rule, unlike a leader. He was impressed by those four Brahmins. He knew that they had been sent by Didda to assist him in matters of the royal court. They established solidarity within the royal court.

These advisors were revered for their wisdom and Mahamardan's role began to diminish. These learned men along with the king improved the state of affairs in the kingdom by leaps and bounds. Abhimanyu was once again respected.

It was the Vasant of AD 972 and by now, Didda had immersed herself in worshiping Shiva. Apart from meditation, the only thing that required her attention was the welfare of the state and its people which comprised of building better infrastructure, creating new villages and constructing temples. Didda also built a town and named it Abhimanyupura. Everyone was surprised that she named it after her son. Deep inside, she missed her son. She then went to Diddapura and consecrated Lord Diddaswami, and a temple for the convenience of travellers who visited from the other parts of the country. In memory of her late husband, she built Kangkanapura, with a sculpture of Lord Vishnu chiselled from white stone, which was also called Diddaswami. She also built a sarai for the traders and travellers to her kingdom. Didda set up another sarai for the convenience of the Brahmin travellers from Lohar and a temple named Simhaswami in the memory of her father. At the junction of the Vitasta and the Sindhu rivers, she built temples and an abode of gods that made the place holy. Didda built a staggering number of sixty-four images of gods keeping in mind the sanctity of the 'Vedic' importance of the number 64.

All this had been fuelling Vasundhara's anger. She had become a prisoner of her own vengeance. Having to watch

Didda rule the hearts without a throne or a scepter devastated her. She felt that the four Brahmins had further infiltrated the palace at Didda's behest and had quietly built a parallel administration further diluting Vasundhara's dominion. If people wanted to address their issues, they would go to Didda instead of coming to the court. She had also seen the ministers go to her for counsel. Most of all, her father went to meet Didda but never sought to meet his daughter. AdityaRaj also requested Didda to return to the palace. Vasundhara, deeply hurt by this, was consumed by the thought of eliminating Didda. This was but an implausible thought considering the loyal Ekangi sena's ironclad security. She presumed that Didda was the reason her husband and father had distanced themselves from her. Vasundhara understood that Didda's real power lay in her people. She thought of ways she could snatch away this power from her. She wanted the masses to turn against their Didda.

A baffled Vasundhara began attending court to ensure that Abhimanyu doesn't lose the throne. She noticed that the four Brahmin advisors were actually intelligent and would only advise in the best interests of the kingdom. Abhimanyu found them extremely able and in whom he could repose his trust. He sought their guidance in hearing the plights of the people who came to the royal court.

Vasundhara thought to artifice a way to oust Didda without being involved. She sought Mahamardan as an aide. They presented a man in the court who had been accused of spying in the kingdom. He stayed in different lodges in the guise of a trader. Vasundhara then accused Didda of exposing the kingdom to an external threat by allowing the construction of those lodges. The man also accepted that Didda supported him in every manner. She then consulted the four Brahmins. On hearing Didda's name, they remained unperturbed. They collectively clarified that there was no past record of her misdeeds; hence, she could not be sent to prison. However, she could be imprisoned wherever she was staying. She would be under strict supervision and all her movements would be closely monitored. She would not be allowed to move around freely, meet anyone or call for anyone.

Vasundhara wanted to imprison Didda but the advisor had given their verdict after they assayed the situation. Vasundhara also observed that the Brahmin advisors took a decision with rectitude. She realized that with them, Abhimanyu could successfully rule the kingdom of Kashmir in future.

Vasundhara could not gauge what Abhimanyu was feeling for Didda. But she could feel the remorse he had for his actions.

That night, Vasundhara and Abhimanyu had a heated argument. Abhimanyu explained to her once again that had Didda wanted to kill her or her son, she had all the means to do so, but she did not. Whatever Didda did was for their good and he did not want to hear a single word against her in the time to come. He warned her that if she repeated any such behaviour, he would be forced to banish her from the kingdom and get Didda back to the palace. Abhimanyu walked out impassively.

Seeing Abhimanyu's aggressive declaration, Vasundhara was enraged. She vied for revenge from Didda. She rushed to the court, sat on the throne and said, 'From now on, if anybody tried meeting Didda or communicating with her in any way, he or she would be put to death without trial.'

Didda and the Bride from Himavat

She hurriedly passed these orders without even consulting Abhimanyu. The four Brahmins advisors opposed this, but she ordered Mahamardan to execute them. Mahamardan immediately obeyed. Vasundhara then fulminated and asked if anybody present in the court had an objection to her order. There was absolute silence.

Vasundhara felt the power of the throne within her. She was at peace with herself. She had chosen the throne after Abhimanyu's hostility and abhorrence towards her. She surmised that she would get rid of anything and anyone who would come between her and the throne. She decided that it will now be her army which would guard Didda. She would get rid of the Ekangi's. If Didda insisted on having her own force around, it would be considered sedition. Didda would now be under the jurisdiction of her court. Vasundhara was the queen and she could do whatever she pleased. The power of the throne had awakened the devil inside Vasundhara.

Didda knew that the accusation of spying by a trader was Vasundhara's doing. For a moment, she even appreciated Vasundhara's thinking and planning by which she had used Didda's advisors against her.

She also applauded the fact that she had planned it so well that Didda got no chance to respond to her. However, nothing affected Didda anymore. Even if Abhimanyu put her behind bars, she would accept it as her destiny.

The next day, Vasundhara's orders spread across the village. People packed their belongings in Valaga village as well. Horse carts left the village and houses were emptied slowly. People said goodbye to Didda and left the village. They sought for her forgiveness and told her that they could not stay with her any longer. Women cried for they had to leave their homes. Very soon, the whole village wore a deserted look. Everything was uprooted. It was only Didda and Valaga who were left behind.

Didda waited to see to what extent would Vasundhara go to get rid of her enemies. She wanted Vasundhara to take extreme steps like this. She was actually testing her. The whole village was deserted but Valaga knew that this silence that prevailed was just a prelude; it was the quiet before the storm.

Very soon, Didda was surrounded by Mahamardan's soldiers. She ordered her Ekangi army, which was moving forth secretively, to stop immediately. She knew she was being watched.

By sunset what transpired in the court had spread like wildfire. People became aware that they were bearing the brunt of the war between Didda and Vasundhara. The killing of the four Brahmin men had not gone down well with them. The masses readied themselves to protest against Vasundhara. They wanted Didda to be readmitted in the kingdom.

However, Vasundhara had ensured that she always was around Abhimanyu to either stop or ensure nothing reached Abhimanyu's ears.

After his squabble with Vasundhara, the king regretted his inability to protect his mother from what was happening. The whole palace was terrorized by Vasundhara and Mahamardan. Everyone knew that if even a word was uttered, they would be killed.

That night, Didda was busy in her prayers when Valaga saw shadows outside the house. She immediately understood that this was an attack on Didda. She tried to tell Didda to get up but Didda could not break her practice and leave her

Didda and the Bride from Himavat 181

mediation in between. She continued to pray with her eyes closed without any fear.

Valaga was unable to find a way to save Didda. She hurriedly decided to seek Abhimanyu's help. In fact, he was the only one who could save Didda from this portentous attack lurking at the moment. She ran frantically towards the palace, though she heard the squelching noises behind her. Mahamardan spotted her while she was entering the palace. By the time, Mahamardan could attack Valaga, a chambermaid yanked Valaga inside her chamber and desperately pleaded Valaga for her help.

'Please get Queen Didda here. All the pandits have been killed. Vasundhara has taken over the kingdom. The king also has been taken hostage and kept under guard.' Valaga was shocked on hearing this. Valaga had to act swiftly in these precarious times. Having stayed in the palace, she knew all the secret paths within the palace. She used this knowledge with great alacrity and tried to escape and narrate Abhimanyu's condition to Didda.

On the other hand, Abhimanyu could not come to terms with the news from informants that Vasundhara has planned to attack his mother. In a fit of rage, he started to walk towards Vasundhara when he heard some noise. Vasundhara entered his room along with Mahamardan. Abhimanyu lost his temper when he saw Vasundhara. He hollered and abused her. He said she could do whatever she wanted but his mother was so brave that she would even defeat death. He told Vasundhara he had lost all respect for her and he wanted her to leave the palace immediately. Hearing this, an infuriated Vasundhara tried to stop Abhimanyu but he pushed her aside and walked out. When Mahamardan saw this, he realized that Abhimanyu would get

Didda back. He saw the throne slipping away from his grip. The cunning Mahamardan followed him and attacked from behind. Abhimanyu did not even get a chance to defend himself.

Vasundhara could not understand what had happened. She blurted, 'Didda will not leave us now. We have killed her son. If we want to save our lives, Didda will have to die. This is open war now. Go kill her.'

However, Mahamardan did not have any courage to carry out the order and face Didda in combat. Instead, he enhanced the security of the palace. Hidden behind the secret door, Valaga saw everything happen in front of her. Her soul wrenched, but, unfortunately, she could do nothing. She was now worried about Didda and how she would break the grave news to her. She took the secret routes to reach the village. It was dawn by then.

Didda came out of her room after concluding her prayers. She saw Valaga sitting quietly amongst the bodies of Mahamardan's soldiers. The Ekangi army had done their job well. They had managed to keep Didda safe.

Valaga didn't know how and what to tell Didda. She broke the news with a heavy heart that Mahamardan had treacherously killed Abhimanyu and that his body laid in Didda's chamber. Didda was speechless. After a long silence, she let out a deep sigh. She trembled with rage as she collected herself and donned her warrior armour once again. She signalled the Ekangi army to begin the ardurous journey toward the palace in a blood-curdling rage.

People took to the streets shouting slogans against Queen Vasundhara. They marched towards the palace, demanding Vasundhara to relinquish her throne and hand over the reigns of Kashmir to Didda. Vasundhara could hear all this sitting in her chamber. She resented Didda's name, but it was all around her.

Seeing the crowds advancing towards the palace, Mahamardan erupted with anger. He ordered his soldiers to attack the masses. But people continued to besiege and surrounded the palace. Just then, Didda attacked the palace along with her Ekangi army.

The soldiers continued to fight bravely, but she entered the palace with a sword in her hand. She saw her son lying dead, exsanguinated in blood. Instead of going near her son, Didda continued to hunt Mahamardan. Scared to his bones, Mahamardan hid in the palace. Didda searched for him like a wounded tigress until she finally spotted him.

Didda did not give him an easy death. She pulled him out and brought him to the palace courtyard. As the soldiers of the Ekangi army held him, she pulled out each strand of his hair and then plucked out his nails. Intermittently, Didda kept looking at Vasundhara's window as she wanted her to see the fate of a murderer.

There was malevolence in Didda's eyes for Vasundhara too.

Mahamardan screamed in agony and Vasundhara could hear his shrills clearly. She looked out of her window and saw Didda chop off every limb, one after the other until he soaked in a fountain of blood. It was a miasma of madness. Vasundhara had never seen anything like this before. For the first time, she saw Didda's rage transform from her meditative self to the 'ranchandi roop'. She knew Didda would slay her too. Vasundhara now was desperate and decided to escape.

She turned around to pick up her son from the cradle, but

he was not there. She rushed back to the window and saw that someone had taken her son and given him to Valaga. Didda was now chopping Mahamardan's shoulders. He was writhing in agony screaming for forgiveness as Didda's blade silenced his cries and his severed head fell off his shoulders and rolled on to the courtyard.

A deafening fury of a mother echoed across the vastness of the palace. The people in the courtyard did not know how to calm Didda's anger. It was not the queen or the warrior they were scared of but a mother whose only son had been slain by the insatiable greed of Vasundhara for the throne of Kashmir.

Vasundhara saw Didda approaching and she was transfixed with fear. She had seen what had happened with Mahamardan. She ran towards the court passing the palace and reached the throne. Didda, with her crippled leg, slowly approached her. She could hear her heavy footsteps. She wanted to shout out for Abhimanyu, but no sound enunciated from her; she was paralysed with fear.

Just then, she spotted Abhimanyu's sword next to the throne. She immediately picked it up, upheld it like a queen and sat on the throne. She was under tremendous duress, something she had never experienced. Just then, she saw Didda standing at the entrance. Didda watched Vansundhara with unflinching eyes. Vasundhara knew she was routed, and her nemesis stood in front of her. She steadied the sword and before anyone could act, pierced herself to an agonizing death.

Didda shook her head and walked towards her chamber, where her son was lying in a pool of blood. Tears rolled down her face. The guilt of leaving the palace gnawed her from within. She held her dead son in her arms recalling all those moments when she held him as a little boy. He had spent his entire childhood in Didda's shadow. Today, Didda was left bereaved with no one to call her own. Didda wailed as she held her son when Valaga placed Abhimanyu's son in her lap. She held her grandson and understood that it was a new beginning for her. It was time that the past was laid to rest.

She gently gave away Abhimanyu to the holy fire and readied herself for a new battle.

Didda saw her life as the epic battle of Kurukshetra. She realized that only the *Bhagwad Gita* could bring her respite. She reached out to BuyaDev and requested him to continue as her spiritual advisor. This time around, BuyaDev taught her the meaning of life through *Bhagwad Gita*. BuyaDev assuaged the turmoil in Didda's life and urged her to march ahead to fulfil her Karma—the promise that she had once made to KshemGupt that she would ensure the well-being of his kingdom. BuyaDev motivated a distraught Didda in the same manner that Lord Krishna had brought back Arjuna from the brink of internal collapse.

9

The Monk Queen and Tunga—the New Army Commander

Didda was aggrieved by the death of her son Abhimanyu. She realized that the kingdom had ebbed to lawlessness again and people had been left to the mercy of the officials. The menace of corruption had returned, and all welfare schemes and justice system had been reduced to a mockery. She moved in the kingdom incognito to assess the situation and found the people grieving and seeking the return of Queen Didda to restore the stability in the entire region. Didda resisted the idea owing to the past taunts on her disability that had scarred her soul deeply. However, the gods had planned an extraordinary destiny for her.

Didda anointed her infant grandson NandiGupt as the next king of Kashmir and agreed to become a regent once again. However, it was not going to be easy. Trouble had already been brewing… Due to the excesses of the officials, the Damars had reunited and had been threatening to overthrow Didda and the infant king. She discovered that many nobles had been conspiring to seize the throne of Kashmir. She banished them from the kingdom in spite of their great influence. Soon, these nobles also rebelled, but a prepared Didda swiftly crushed them winning over the Brahmin supporters who had initially supported the nobles.

Thakkana, one of the most powerful rulers of a neighbouring kingdom of Shahi descent, joined the revolt. Didda chose Yashodhar, one of her trusted commanders to counter him. He was amongst the Brahmin warlords whom Didda had an alliance with. Yashodhar crushed Thakkana in a brutal war but allowed him to retain his kingdom when the defeated king sought mercy. On his way back, Yashodhar was surrounded by his legions who roused his ambition for power. In a drunken state that night in his victory camp, Yashodhar lost to his better senses and announced to overthrow Queen Didda. He believed that the kingdom needed a strong male king and not a lame queen. He and his legions hatched a plan to take the kingdom by surprise upon their return. Yashodhar returned to the kingdom expecting a hero's welcome but found the royal guards waiting for him asking him to surrender. A shocked Yashodhar immediately revolted and many nobles joined him. Both the armies clashed at the gates of the valley as the queen watched over the ramparts of her palace.

She was saddened by the betrayal from one of her 'trusted' men. Some of the greatest and bravest men had betrayed her, all because she was a woman. They failed to see her as a leader and a creator of a strong kingdom from a disintegrated system left by her husband.

This was perhaps the toughest revolt Didda faced at this age since Yashodhar and his men thwarted Didda's army and were on the verge of plundering the palace. She had to act fast as Yashodhar's army was now within a striking distance of the palace. He and his men looked at Didda and broke into a sinister laughter—they knew the coveted throne was within their reach. They had almost started their celebrations when the palace door opened, and the battlefield rattled as if thunder had stuck.

Didda rode out with her Ekangi's. Her menacing anger and sword cut through whatever came in her way. Blinded with rage, she hollered the war cry, 'Har Har Mahadev'. Watching her, many of the fleeing men suddenly returned to the battlefield. Before Yashodar could realize what was happening, Didda's sword was at his throat. Yashodhar and his men were captured, and they trembled recalling the rumours of Didda and her wrath as a witch queen. Yashodhar and his men stood in line to be publicly hanged in front of the Srinagaram palace as Didda watched the proceedings from the ramparts.

After a long time, Didda was visiting her parents through the same dense jungles where she had once found love and husband KshemGupt. Lost in her thoughts, she suddenly sensed something unusual. Her heart began to thump. She had an eternal connection with the wilderness of those jungles. Something was in the air that she recognized; the jungle was far more serene than she would have preferred when all of a sudden, a flock of birds took to the air. 'Something must have disturbed them,' she thought.

Didda gauged her surroundings without alarming her men. Didda swiftly reached for her sword, but just before she could raise an alarm, an arrow fell a soldier to the ground. Before anyone could react, a volley of arrows began to rain on the brigade. The palanquin carrying Didda tumbled over as the porters fell to the arrows. Didda found herself in the middle of an ambush. She saw her men being killed by invisible marksmen. Didda too was injured and trapped inside her palanquin.

The arrows suddenly stopped and Didda struggled to get out of the palanquin. She saw a few men emerge from the forest killing the injured.

'Stop it, you cowards,' Didda screamed at the marauders.

'Stop it, I say,' Didda struggled and felt miserable because of her disability. She was infuriated with rage as the killers continued butchering the men as if they were lambs.

Didda screamed as she dug her fingers into the soil, trying to push herself out from underneath the palanquin. She saw them, and they had a smile as they began to walk towards her. In that moment of weakness, Didda wept from within, not for the sake of her life but for her inability to push out of that immensely heavy palanquin. It reminded her of the disability which otherwise never deterred Didda. Trapped and on the ground, she recalled how her cousins would push her around and how they all would hurl abuses of 'Langdi... Langdi' (meaning limp). Inches away from certain death, Didda composed and prepared herself for the coldness of a coward's blade to rip her neck open.

The group of mercenaries surrounded Didda and one of them came forward. Hiding behind a veil, he seemed mesmerized by Didda. Perhaps he was overwhelmed thinking this was Didda, the crippled queen, the witch queen. A flurry of thoughts was racing through his mind. 'Was she really a witch or just a myth? How could she be trapped like an ordinary woman?' He raised his sword to end her agony. And then something happened, and he stopped with his sword aloft. Didda stared at him, waiting for the ominous moment to end it all. It was the longest moment of her life—the killer seemingly still, staring back at Didda. Those moments seemed frozen as she watched the expressions of the killer change. His eyes were full of disbelief and in an instant; his sword dropped and pierced the ground just missing Didda's face.

'You are a witch,' mumbled the killer.

'Witch,' he said again as blood began to ooze through his chest. Horrified, he held his hand against his chest and fell with a thump.

Before anyone realized what had happened, arrows began to pierce the remaining soldiers.

Still trapped underneath the palanquin, Didda was helpless. In just a few moments, she had travelled a million miles across the worlds and crossed the bridge between life and imminent death. What perturbed her the most, in those few moments, was the fear of dying a lame death; and, the words of the killer—'You are a witch'.

All of a sudden, one by one, all the assailants fell and she saw the silhouette of a man appear. He emerged out of the dark shadows of the thick forest and fought the remaining killers by himself. It was surreal for Didda. One thought pervaded her mind—would he save her or was he another killer? Didda was still not sure. However, she was certain of one fact that he was an ace swordsman with an extremely able body. He was raw in his moves, yet very lethal; he seemed to be a master of swordcraft and physical combat. Yet again, fate had twisted the path to her redemption. The man came to Didda and began moving the heavy walnut palanquin. Having pushed it over, he reached out to Didda.

'Are you fine? You seem hurt.'

'Who are you? Didda attempted to get up but a severe spasm made her shriek in pain and she fell to the ground.

The saviour immediately reached out and lifted her.

'Who are you? Even though in agony, she asked him again.

'Tunga Kaashi,' he replied.

'I am a local herdsman here and live with my brothers in the jungle,' he continued.

'Herdsman!' Didda exclaimed, trying to compose herself. She got hold of her artificial foot.

'Didda, Raani Didda,' other herdsmen almost shouted in exhilaration.

Didda asked them to calm down as she walked up to her slain soldiers. All of them stood quietly looking at the dead bodies, some still oozing blood. Didda was overwhelmed with grief and pain. She loved each soldier as her own, and in them, she always saw herself. The entire ambush and witnessing the death of her warriors unable to do anything had drained her. She settled down alongside her motionless warriors. Soon, the pain was becoming unbearable for Didda. Everything around her was adding to her nausea and she felt the ground caving in and fell unconscious.

Dawn was breaking when Didda regained her consciousness. She had slept well for a few hours and felt better. However, she found herself in an unusual place. It was a kotha; usually, the nomads around Lohar and Pir Panjal dwelled in such makeshift huts. She knew she was safe as her sword was next to her. She recalled the events, reliving those painful moments that antedated a few hours ago and her handicap that caused the death of her soldiers; or so, she thought.

Soon, Tunga walked in, hands clasped, and head bowed in

reverence. He explained to Didda how he had seen some unusual men in his area laying an ambush. He had told his brothers their movements but they asked him to mind his own business—no one wanted to mess with royal soldiers. Tunga, however, kept a close watch and then he saw them attack Didda's convoy. He couldn't hold himself back when he realized that the killers wanted to kill Didda. Little did he know that not only was he about to save his queen, but also alter the course of his own life. Maybe it was destined to be this way. No one knew this act of random and selfless bravery had set in motion a chain of events that would see the transformation of a herdsman into one of the greatest military generals of the northern territories.

Didda was truly impressed by his bravery and felt her heart melt for the first time in years with the selfless act of a truly brave man. There was something alluring about Tunga. His reticent composure provided a sharp contrast to his bravery and selflessness. In an age of deceit, greed and hunger for power, Tunga stood out as a rare breed of men that Didda craved to find. Didda ordered two brothers of Tunga's to resume their duties in Kashmir and another brother was commissioned to Lohar with the news of her welfare and reinforcements. Didda spent two days wandering around the jungles, at least that is what Tunga thought. Didda wasn't just wandering, she was thinking about the hidden enemy. Could it be Phalgun? Would he dare such an ambush? The attack had left a scathing impact on Didda's mind.

Soon, it was time to travel and settle the rumours of her death. This would reinforce Didda as the invincible warrior queen. For many, it would add credence to the rumours of her having supernatural powers but for some, she would emerge as the witch queen.

The Monk Queen and Tunga—the New Army Commander

Didda took a major decision during her stay with Tunga. She decided to take Tunga to Lohar and introduce him to her brothers as the man who saved her life. But back in Srinagaram, she did the unthinkable by appointing Tunga as the military commander.

Tunga proved his prowess soon enough, not just in combat but also in matters of administration. He was a natural leader—someone who had the ability to delve deep into a critical matter and emerge with a solution. However, it was not as simple as it seemed for Tunga. A simple herdsman was at the altars of great power and social transformation much beyond his imagination.

Tunga had begun to believe in the extraordinary abilities of Didda and realized it was best for him to support her endeavours. It was not just her extraordinary capabilities, but being a man, it was difficult not to fall in love with her. Tunga found himself enamoured of Didda; thus, his internal struggle too had begun. Destiny never failed to surprise Didda. Would Tunga walk in the footsteps of Narvahan or would he avoid the pitfall? Destiny seemed to have laid the chessboard between Didda and Tunga for both to play.

The court was full of powerful men with deep-rooted prejudices and they had just begun accepting a woman as their queen. Accepting Tunga as their military commander was hard to swallow. Not just the courtiers, but Didda's own blood instigated a rebellion against Tunga. The most important instigator was Didda's nephew Vigraharaja who found strong allies in the Brahmins of Awantipur and Varaheshwara.

Fasting was always the strongest tool of Brahmins of Kashmir, strong enough to have the crown bow to them. Both Awantipur and Varaheshwara were critical seats of the Brahmin power. They controlled the revered Vishnu and Shiva temple sites. They were not just custodians of the two powerful sites of Vedic power, but also the guardians of vast treasuries full of jewels, silver, copper and gold. Support of the Brahmins directly meant the kingdom was bolstered with financial assistance by way of gold required to run the administration, and appointment as well as maintenance of the armies.

Vigraharaja played the sinister game that the kingdom of Kashmir had witnessed many times in the past. Right from the times of ParvGupt, Kashmir's throne had been seeking blood. However, this was a different time, a different era. Didda was the guardian of the throne and her presence alone was enough to pulverize enemy threats. Vigraharaja needed something more than the Brahmins. He needed someone who could weaken Didda emotionally.

Vigraharaja persuaded an impressionable NandiGupt to side with him in this rebellion against Tunga. BhimGupt was unsure, as he knew going against Didda would mean death. However, Vigraharaja indoctrinated and persuaded BhimGupt to lend his support. BhimGupt knew he could never control the throne of Srinagaram while Didda was around, and with the appointment of Tunga as a military commander, his control had attenuated.

BhimGupt had been ousted from his position, but he was still fearful of Didda. With BhimGupt as his ally, Vigraharaja believed he could disseminate not just Tunga but Didda as well. He needed more support and decided to cahoot a circle of powerful and influential men who could form this allegiance. Eventually, this allegiance roused BhimGupt to order the extermination of Tunga.

BhimGupt's fears came true and Didda's secret army

The Monk Queen and Tunga—the New Army Commander 195

briefed her about the plot to kill the newly-appointed military commander. After Narvahan's suicide, she had learnt to protect her loyalists at all times. Didda sent her royal guards to keep Tunga safe; however, attempts on his life were made.

It became increasingly difficult for Didda to keep Tunga close and yet safe. Didda realized that Tunga too would eventually fall to either the vices or the virtues of men. She had lost a great friend in Narvahan and now she didn't want to lose Tunga.

Didda was still considered a beauty of her time and yearned for the love of a man, but being the queen, this was not permissible since the kingdom needed able hands to stabilize and cover lost grounds from the turmoil it had endured. Tunga was the one but Didda had to make a difficult decision. Tunga would sooner or later die if she continued to keep him in Kashimir. Eventually, Didda sent Tunga to assist her brother in Lohar. For days she felt a strange void; she also questioned her Lord, 'Why must I always live without the people I love?'

Central Asia was abuzz with various communities at war in an effort to extend their frontiers. Islam was establishing itself across Turkey and Syria. Jerusalem, the Holy Land, was under Muslim dominance. Didda recalled her grandfather's political learnings. Christianity was on a decline ever since AD 500, and anytime now, they would reorganize and countermand the situation. Jerusalem started to beckon a revolution. On many occasions, BheemShah had shared his knowledge of world political developments with Didda.

Didda needed someone as strong as Tunga without facing the risk of losing him to conspirators and traitors. At that time, she only had Rakka to lead her army, but Rakka too was not untouched by greed. It was ironic that these powerful men were humbled in front of Didda. Various concoctions that Rakka had got himself addicted to were taking a toll on his body. Who had been once a powerful warlord and had the right to challenge Didda, was now a recluse. His hands could no longer hold his valour or the sword. Rakka was dying a painful death without anyone knowing about it. What was killing him faster was his guilt. However, Didda relied on Rakka to handle not just the impending threats from Central Asian warlords, but also internal threats of a Damar uprising.

'All could never be well'—this adage was so apt for Didda's regime. In coming days, Rakka was found dead in his chamber.

Didda was left alone and she could see the Damars uniting against her. At that time, she did something preposterous. A word was sent out to recall Phalgun who had been living in exile. Phalgun had transformed and effectively subdued the Damars.

It was not just the Damars, the plains of Central Asia, the Mediterranean and Europa—everything was bursting at the seams. The world was reorganizing itself; good was paving way for the unscrupulous and the brazen. Borders were constantly changing, dynasties were fading away and kingdoms were falling, making way for the new ones to rise. It was a new world changing its course, not far from the ironclad boundaries of Kashmir. The Ekangi's intelligence was continuously briefing Didda and apprising her of the implications. A new world was emerging in the tenth century and Didda was concerned about the fate of her own world.

She knew the threat from new religions, such as Islam, expanding their roots across Africa and Asia, while Islam itself was facing a change in power dynamics and was on the verge

The Monk Queen and Tunga—the New Army Commander

of entering a new phase.

Even before Mahmud, his father Abu Sabuktigin, a Samanid Turkic slave governor in the Afghan mountains, had made himself independent of his masters as their central power declined. Mahmud then expanded into Buyid territory in western Iran, identifying himself staunchly with Sunni Islam. It was ruling Iran, which gave a Muslim ruler true prestige that Mahmud sought to establish himself.

The Samanid dynasty (819–999) stemmed from a local family appointed by the Abbasids to govern Bukhara and Samarkand. Gradually, the Samanids absorbed the domains of the rebellious Tahirids and Saffarids in northeastern Iran and reduced the Saffarids to a small state in Sistan. The Samanids, relying on Turkic slave troops, also managed to contain the migratory pastoralist Turkic tribes who continually pressed on Iran from across the Oxus River.

Didda recalled that, way back in 950s, they had even managed to convert some of these Turkic tribes into Islam, and BheemShah was concerned about these developments. Ekangi's intelligence seemed to believe that Islam eventually would turn to cross the Hindu Kush range. The Samanids also fostered the development of a second Islamicate language of high culture—the New Persian language. It combined the grammatical structure and vocabulary of spoken Persian with that of Arabic, the existing language of high culture in Iran. The then-emerging poet Ferdowsī brought Iran's ancient heroic lore, and its hero, Rustam, into Islamic literature and into the identity of self-consciously Iranian Muslims. He began to compose a poem under the rule of the Samanids; but he dedicated the finished work to a dynasty that had meanwhile replaced them—

the Ghaznavids. It was not the just the geo-political reorientation but also a period of new languages and cultural identities. Didda was anxious for the sustenance of her unique culture, language and heritage if she was no longer in control.

In addition, in Africa, from the eighth century, Islam had started spreading gradually south in the oases of the Sahara trade routes. Africa was the first region into which Islam was carried by merchants rather than armies. It spread down the well-established trade routes of the East Coast in which the coastal towns of the Red Sea (the very heart of Islam) played a major part.

The way Islam was surging, Didda realized that in coming decades, Muslims would rule many of the trade routes and kingdoms.

Even Europe was not untouched. Didda even remembered how it all began in AD 955, just a few years after she moved to Kashmir after her marriage. The news of the Battle of Lechfeld saw a decisive victory for Otto I the Great, the king of the Germans, over the Hungarian Harka Bulcsu and the chieftains Lehel and Sur. Around the same era in AD 960, palace guards had surrounded their commander and demanded that he became the emperor of China. The commander agreed, but only if they vowed to obey him and not plunder, not harm the citizens or the ruling family they were overthrowing. The troops agreed. The new emperor Taizu began the Song dynasty. It had amazed both Didda and KshemGupt, and they wondered if loyalty of that kind could be found in Kashmir.

In AD 965, Kievan Rus, the Slavic tribes of Eastern Europe attacked and defeated the Khazar dynasty that ruled over the Khazaria kingdom, which included the geographic regions of southern Russia, northern Caucasus, eastern Ukraine, Crimea, western Kazakhstan and north-western Uzbekistan.

In AD 980, wealthy landowners in Japan freed themselves from paying taxes. The government made little in revenues and stopped supporting a national army. The wealthy landowners consolidated their lands into a single administrative unit, creating their own armies. The men hired for these armies were known as samurai (men who serve) or bushi (warriors). Didda would often scoff at them, believing they aped her Ekangi's.

With so much turmoil all around her, Didda realized that she needed a steady male king for the kingdom. She could sense that it was just a matter of time that people and corrupt ministers would revolt, and Damars and other warlords from the upper reaches would soon swallow the kingdom of her husband. Now Didda had to make some radical decisions, these decisions could strengthen the kingdom and in so doing she risked going down in the annals of history as a witch queen.

Didda did the unthinkable, in AD 973. Compelled by the inability of NandiGupt to manage the Kingdom, she 'disposed' of NandiGupt. In AD 975, she anointed her youngest grandson, Bhimagupta as the king, with herself as the regent.

With the sudden demise of Phalgun, the chief minister, Didda, once again, was left alone amidst a band of conniving circumstances and men who were prone to betrayal. Things took an untoward turn when the young king Bhimagupta died prematurely in AD 981 in mysterious circumstances. This re-enforced the old belief among courtiers that Didda was behind his death and that she was a witch queen. With the death of the young king, Didda decided that it was time for her to ascend the throne.

10

Didda's Final Tryst with Destiny and the Sultan of Ghaznavi

Didda once again sat on the throne of Kashmir. Like earlier, she had several enemies within the palace who did not accept to be commanded by a woman and these very perpetrators plotted many attempts on her life. Rulers of different kingdoms believed her to be vulnerable and intermittently attacked her. She always had the onus of defending her kingdom.

This time again the power did not come with any fewer challenges. There was a huge imbalance within the kingdom and she had many enemies who did not want her to wear the crown. What made it even more difficult was that this time Didda was alone. She had no loyalist and trusted commanders by her side. There was no one to share her grief and her insecurities, no one to shoulder her burden and support her endeavours in the hour of need. Everyone whom she trusted in, believed in or relied on had left her. Having seen so many kings die and kingdoms ravaged, one after the other, Didda's resolve broke from within. It was just her commitment towards the kingdom and her oath to protect it that motivated her to be strong and continue with the same strength which she was known for.

Didda had to do it all alone this time. Since childhood, she had Valaga by her side; then there was KshemGupt; later, there was Narvahan; there was her son; then there was even Phalgun to share her responsibilities with and who guided her through tough situations. Later, she found Tunga. In this time of turmoil and loneliness, Didda again had no alternative and summoned Tunga. He was reassigned to Srinagaram and was made the prime minister and the military commander. He efficiently took over the responsibilities and filled a huge void with his presence.

His skills and abilities were not hidden from anyone. Despite being a mere herdsman, he was very capable of administrating the military and the ministries as well. His previous stint in the capital had already shut many mouths who believed he was not good enough to be in that position. Unlike the previous occasion, this time his appointment did not spark any outrage. Everyone knew he had Didda's back and that the queen was even more powerful now than ever.

The biggest challenge for Tunga was to bring peace to the kingdom and make things easy for Didda. He took over certain responsibilities to restore law and order and during this process set right the troublemakers. Tunga went on to quell successfully many a difficult situation, crushing the rebellion in the western parts (Rajouri) of the kingdom.

Tunga managed to seize them with a mere threat and a display of power. There was discontent amongst the Damars and they were a cause of trouble for a long time. Didda was concerned about this and a huge effort was required to tackle them. Tunga's application of his military prowess and intelligence subdued this crisis, thus befitting his commanding presence not only in the kingdom but also on the battlefront. He devised a plan that helped Didda reform some policies to please the Damars and used power wherever necessary. By resolving this issue, he became the harbinger of military and diplomatic acumen.

The royal court sought the new military commander's advice in critical situations. Queen Didda along with her Military Commander Tunga became a formidable force in the region. Tunga not only became the most powerful person in the kingdom but also came close to Didda.

The image of a poor herdsman who came to her rescue when her life was in imminent danger could never go away from Didda's mind. She was indebted, and, in a way, she owed her life to him. She believed she was able to serve her destiny because Tunga saved her from the clutches of death. Some believed that the gratitude was turning into love. With the presence that Tunga held in her life, courtiers began to believe that Didda had finally found peace. Didda on the contrary never clarified these doubts; she didn't have to. This time the reason was different; Narvahan's death had silenced this particular aspect of her life. In her last days, Valaga raised the topic of Tunga, as only she could. Valaga being a close friend and confidante asked Didda, 'Do you love Tunga? If you do, you should marry him.'

Didda was not enraged this time, but she didn't express any emotion.

'If I marry him, won't Destiny take him away too?' she murmured.

Didda's Final Tryst with Destiny and the Sultan of Ghaznavi

Valaga understood her trepidations.

She realized that somewhere deep in her heart, she had the fear of losing him to the maleficences of deceit, power and betrayal that Didda had seen all through her life.

On that very night, Valaga passed away and Didda lost her last and closest confidante from the old guard, but her spirit always remained with Didda. She never believed that Valaga was gone. Didda with Tunga's support faced the predicaments and challenges encountered by the kingdom.

But there was a calamity about to befall Kashmir and destroy it.

A typhoon was set to come from across the mountains. It was predicted that it would damage not just Kashmir but the entire Hindustan. This typhoon would shake the foundations of this peaceful culture that was just coming out of its own turmoil after ages. It would change the course of history. A typhoon called Ghaznavi.

After the death of Didda's maternal grandfather, he had relegated the throne to Jaipal, who was not from his dynasty. He ruled the Hindu Shahi from AD 64 to 101. It was a matter of disappointment for Didda that when Mahmud Ghaznavi's father, Sabuktigin, attacked Jaipal, he surrendered meekly. This resulted in the treaty that compelled Jaipal to surrender Peshawar as well which went into the hands of the Turks. Having the Turks in Peshawar posed the risk of an Islamic invasion into the three states of Kabul, Kashmir and Loharin.

Didda had relations with both the states of Kabul and Loharin. Because of Jaipal, Kabul Shahi saw the dawn of a new lineage. A spineless and venal Jaipal had a different modus operandi and he felt Didda was no longer his concern.

Didda, the warrior, knew that Abu Mansur Subuktigin would have apprehensions in attacking Kashmir, but he could certainly attack Loharin. Didda, being a brilliant visionary and a wise statesman, understood the geo-political imbalances. She joined hands with Loharin. This was a direct message to Sabuktigin; if he confronted Loharin, he would be directly engaging with Didda. She also intimated the Kabul rulers of her support in case of a Turkish invasion.

Sabuktigin was well aware of Didda's power. Stories of her bravery and courage had proliferated in the whole of Iran. Sabuktigin understood the implications and was wise enough in keeping his distance from these three states. This gambit of Didda kept the Turks away from these three states for 20 years.

But at the same time, it was understood that finding the rightful successor of Kashmir's throne was imperative.

She realized that she had begun to age. Didda had caused so much pain to her body and mind to protect herself and the welfare of Kashmir that it had taken a toll on her health.

Didda received intelligence reports of radical geo-political turmoil in the Central Asian plains. The small kingdom of Ghaznavi, across the mountain ranges, was on the verge of disintegration and the elder prince had banished Mahmud.

Without a kingdom, Mahmud was on the run with a small army and he was vanquishing the smaller tribes and kingdoms in order to gather a vast army to regain his hold in Ghaznavi and kill his brother. Mahmud was continuously pillaging them with the primary objective of collecting the spoils, gold and jewels to support a vast rebellion.

Didda realized that it would not be long before he turned his eye on Kashmir. He would consider it to be a vulnerable

Didda's Final Tryst with Destiny and the Sultan of Ghaznavi

target, and an easy route to enter the land of immense wealth and resources. Didda knew that a woman on a throne would lure and make a megalomaniac like him believe he would easily be able to defeat and annex the kingdom of Kashmir.

This was a serious concern weighing on Didda. She knew she had the wherewithal to crush him, but her major concern was her health. She knew she was waning. She needed a comprehensive plan to secure her kingdom from the foreign onslaught.

Another concern for Didda was Vigraharaja. He had made a few attempts to take control of the throne of her paternal kingdom of Loharin and was claiming his authority over it. Didda came up with an idea. She thought of a way to resolve both the issues at the same time.

The time had come to choose a new ruler for Kashmir as well as her paternal kingdom.

Didda's emphasis was not on her bloodline to stake the claim to the kingdom, instead, she wanted a king who would be able to take her place, someone who would have similar qualities as hers and would take her legacy forward. She wanted to choose a candidate who was worthy of being a king of the kingdom.

Didda announced, 'A competition will be organized in a few days' time and the winner will be chosen as the new king.' She also invited young men from her paternal family to participate.

The competition comprised of strategic warfare, swordsmanship, archery and horse-riding. Young men saw this as a grand opportunity and prepared for it. No one wanted to lose this golden chance.

Soon, the day of the competition arrived, and people from

both the kingdoms gathered in the arena to see the young men compete. Everyone was eager to see the future king of Kashmir. They were also keen to know how Queen Didda was going to adjudicate the best amongst them.

Didda arrived with her Military Commander Tunga. Everyone stood and greeted her. Didda signalled for the competition to commence. Attendants entered the arena with a huge vault full of fruits. It was placed in the center and the participants were ordered to grab them in maximum numbers. This was the 'challenge'. The participants had to use any means they could to grab the maximum number of fruits. The boys started grabbing the fruits and fighting with one another. The arena was filled with loud clangouring of swords, while arrows cut through the air, amidst vociferous roars of the princes curdling for each other's blood. Everyone fought fiercely but one.

Meanwhile, Prince Samgramraja stood calmly in a corner and did not engage in any physical fight. He was rousing others to fight and smartly got rid of everyone else and then claimed to have the maximum number of fruits.

Didda was impressed by his tactics and political acumen.

She then announced her decision, 'I adopt and name Samgramraja as the heir to the kingdom of Kashmir while the throne of Lohar will belong to Vigraharaja.'

She organized a public ceremony and said to Samgramraja and Tunga, 'I want you both to take a solemn oath that you would always work together and protect the kingdom.'

'We pledge to protect the kingdom together and will never let you down, Our Queen,' said Tunga and Samgramraja together.

Everyone welcomed the decision and the arena was filled with the clarion roars of *'Rani Didda ki Jai'* and 'Praise be to Queen Didda'.

From that moment both Samgramraja and Tunga worked together. Samgramraja elevated Tunga as his prime minister. There were many who disliked the selection of Samgramraja and considered him weak. Tunga intervened and took steps to quieten the discord. They brought back stability to the kingdom by working in tandem.

Kashmir, once again, enjoyed the days of prosperity. All social, economic and political issues were settled and peace returned to the kingdom. People were happy with the new regime and heaped praises for Samgramraja and Tunga. Their respect for their Queen Didda also increased, as they believed that once again she had sacrificed herself for the good of the kingdom. The label of the witch queen was slowly being excoriated by the masses.

Didda was also happy for she could see the kingdom becoming more powerful after the wise distribution of powers. Her biggest concern was whether Samgramraja would abide by his oath and continue working with Tunga? Will he respect her words after he is seated with power? Samgramraja did nothing wrong to raise Didda's worries. She was content that both of them respected her and devoted themselves to serve the kingdom. She knew that they would have been unable to administer and manage the kingdom without each other's support. She mentored them and made sure that conspirators and traitors were never able to create rifts between them.

With each passing day, Didda could feel her age taking a toll on her body. On knowing about Didda's ill health, AbhinavGupt visited her. He arrived early morning and greeted Didda with a smile. Didda was pleased to see him after a long time. However, his eyes said something different, as if he was holding back some information. Didda could sense it.

'I am really proud of you, Didda. You have come a long way since we first met,' said AbhinavGupt.

'This is all because of your blessing, Your Holiness,' she replied with utter humbleness.

'Who am I to bless anyone? I am just a well-wisher. The one who blesses is the Almighty. It is the Shiva. Everything that happens is His command. He is the saviour; He is the destructor; He is everything from aadi to the anth; He is life; He is death; He is the Shakti.'

'You have come this far to tell me the might of Lord Shiva, have you?' she asked.

'No, I have come to tell you that it has been a long time since you have kept yourself busy with the throne and its people. Now, the time has come…'

'Time for what, Your Holiness?' Didda asked with concern.

'It is time to dedicate yourself to the Lord, to give as much time as you can to worship Him who has given you everything.'

'I know, Your Holiness. I cannot forget what the Lord has given me. The Lord made me meet you. You were Shiva's messenger in my life. It was because of you that I got Abhimanyu, it was because of you that my life changed. It was because of you that I got the respect and the right I deserved.'

'I had told you earlier, Didda, that it was not me. I could see that you are my Lord's blessed creation, and I felt it was my Lord's order to help you. Now, I think its time for you to do something for the Lord. I request you to do a Mahayajna to seek the Lord's blessings.'

'If you say so, Your Holiness, I will do it. But, why all this suddenly?'

'Sometimes we should not delay and leave things for tomorrow. Sometimes we should do things as soon as we feel them. You never know what tomorrow will be like. You never know where you will be tomorrow.'

These words of AbhinavGupt made things very clear to Didda. She understood the purpose of his visit. Soon, the preparations for the Mahayajna were made and after conducting the yajna, AbhinavGupt left. But before leaving, he had conveyed to Didda what he wanted to. Didda understood that her time had come. She had to depart. But, even in such trying times, Didda did not forget her responsibility. She summoned Tunga and Samgramraja and asked them to promise her that they will continue to support each other forever, irrespective of the circumstances, irrespective of her presence or absence; they would protect the kingdom and its people with their blood and sweat. She also made them aware of the serious threat that was to come in future. She told them that they had to be prepared to face Mahmud of Ghaznavi.

'You know, I only have a few days left of my life. I am happy that I have given the custody of this kingdom in very good hands, but I have one last wish that I want you to fulfil.'

'Tell us, mother. We have never let you down and will make sure that we live up to your expectations again,' said Samgramraja.

'I want you to protect this land from Mahmud. Make sure that he is never able to put his venomous foot on this land of Shiva.'

'We promise you, Our Queen. We will never let Mahmud enter our kingdom,' Tunga promised holding her hand.

Soon, he felt that Didda's hand turned cold and her eyes closed. This was the moment. With an assurance from her heir Samgramraja that her legacy will remain alive after her, Didda passed away at the age of 79, in AD 1003. An extraordinary queen had taken her final bow after seeing the triumphs and tribulations of Kashmir and restoring her glory for now and its future.

With Didda's hand in his, Tunga broke down. He could not believe that his Didda had left him. It was the first time that the palace of Srinagaram witnessed their braveheart military commander weeping like a child. Samgramraja, too, wailed at the loss of his mentor. Suddenly, the weight of Kashmir's crown on his young shoulders was extremely overwhelming.

The land of Kashmir felt a void within as they saw Didda enter the kingdom above.

It was time for Didda to end all her miseries and begin her ascent to meet her Lord, her Shiva. The queen—who was believed to be a witch by many, a murderer who was responsible for regicide and a being with supernatural powers—had finally, in her death, broken the shackles of prejudice and misconceptions only to be longed, loved and remembered as the great Queen Didda.

People came from far across the kingdom and gathered in Srinagaram to get a glimpse of their queen for the last time. Queen Didda was given a collective farewell and her adopted son Samgramraja, the heir to the kingdom of Kashmir, gave fire to her pyre. People still believed that Didda would resurrect herself from a samadhi using her tantric powers. People stayed

Didda's Final Tryst with Destiny and the Sultan of Ghaznavi

for days in front of the palace, waiting for Didda to rise again. AbhinavGupt asked Samgramraja to release her soul and her ashes into Vitasta. The warrior who rose from the waters of Vitasta went back in peace.

AbhinavGupt anointed Samgramraja as the king and Tunga as his prime minister. This historic moment marked the beginning of Lohar dynasty in Kashmir with Samgramraja as their first king. Samgramraja took charge of the kingdom and fared well on Didda's expectations. The kingdom expanded far deep and wide from west to east.

But in AD 1013 came the enemy whom Didda had already foreseen. Mahmud of Ghaznavi attacked the Shahi kingdom. Samgramraja and Tunga were ready to slaughter the enemies. Didda had already sharpened them to take this enemy to task.

The new invader was unlike any other enemy they had battled. He was brutal, fierce and had no rules but to win on the battlefield. His war tactics were different, his weapons were different, and he proved tough to win over. To aid the Shahi King, Trilochanpal, Tunga himself took a large battalion into the war zone.

A war room was established, and it was decided that Tunga would take a defensive position at a vantage point. Just as the plan was about to be executed, Tunga realized its shortcomings. It dawned upon Tunga that Mahmud, being a megalomaniac and arrogant, would presume that the royal forces would only act defensively in response to his barbaric army.

Tunga carefully scrutinized the situation and decided to launch an unexpected attack by surprising the enemy; something that Ghaznavi would not have imagined even in his vivid dreams. Tunga ordered his army to march forward and attack. The sheer surprise of the royal forces attacking with such fierceness shocked Mahmud's army. Tunga's battalion was ruthless and the battlefield was soaked in blood.

The region had never witnessed such a war before. This was the war to save a culture, a civilization, and their land from slaughter at the hands of a barbaric enemy; it was a war that would be etched in the annals of history. Tunga was fighting like the primordial incarnation of Rudra himself. It felt like Didda's spirit showered her blessings on him, protecting him from the enemy.

As the long battle ensued, the enemies found it hard to stay strong. Finally, Mahmud's army could not withstand the royal forces and fled. Tunga became the saviour of the land, saving it from Mahmud's attempt to invade Kashmir. The news spread deep into the veins of Asiatic plane making Kashmir into a powerful force that could countermand tyrannical oppression from the worst of enemies in the region.

History again repeated itself and Tunga found himself on precarious grounds. As time passed, a rift insinuated between King Samgramraja and Tunga. This was no ordinary situation. The very foundation that Didda considered to be unshakable had cracked at the centre. Things reached to such an extent that Samgramraja decided to exterminate his supreme commander and his solemn oath was moored with his lust for power.

Tunga and his son were treacherously attacked by none other than Tunga's brother along with the king's henchmen.

The land of Kashmir once more bore the pain of losing their finest men and its two protectors. Venal politics had taken away two honest servants of the great land.

Just as Kashmir was entering a golden phase of peace and

Didda's Final Tryst with Destiny and the Sultan of Ghaznavi 213

prosperity, the news of Mahmud of Ghaznavi preparing another attack on Kashmir reached Samgramraja. This time it would be with even greater vengeance and a stronger army than the previous one.

Danger knocked on the doors of the kingdom. The future looked precarious not just for Kashmir but for the entire Hindustan. The only beacon of hope that could save it from the brutality was Samgramraja. He was forewarned by Didda over the period and had prepared himself well for this eventuality. Thus, he was ready to face Ghaznavi.

However, this time around, Tunga wasn't there to lead the army. Samgramraja realized this and took charge of the army himself. He commanded the troops and led the march against Ghaznavi's army.

Once again, a brutal battle was fought. Thousands of men died. The valley was besieged in a river of blood of the men from both the sides. Ghaznavi had come prepared with an array of new weapons, not just arrows and swords. Samgramraja found it difficult to retaliate, but still, motivated his troops to fight until their last breath. Mahmud of Ghaznavi was beaten again and fled. Once again, Kashmir had proved to be a mighty shield for Hindustan, which was protected by the celestial grace of its Queen Didda.

Ghaznavi, after losing yet another battle, was so humiliated by this defeat that he never attempted to attack Kashmir again. He, later, entered India through the border kingdom of Gujarat by Toshmaidan and plundered India.

The military foundation laid by Didda had crushed Ghaznavi's plans not once, but twice. No other kingdom in Hindustan could ever repeat this act because none of the other kingdoms had Didda as their warrior queen.

The crippled girl, who was born in the kingdom of Lohar, rose to become a queen in a kingdom that was forever besieged in turmoil. A little girl who had learned from her childhood that a woman can be as strong as she wanted to. She laid a strong foundation for Kashmir, which was cherished for eras and her blessings always protected the kingdom from every trouble that came towards it.

Through the chasm of history, Didda's brilliance came alive irrespective of the seismic planes that Kashmir finds itself on.

This is my story of hers!